THE FRIDAY
HARBOR MURDERS

ALSO BY DOLORES WEEKS

The Cape Murders

THE FRIDAY HARBOR MURDERS

a novel of suspense

Dolores Weeks

Dodd, Mead & Company
NEW YORK

The characters and situations in this book are entirely fictitious and
bear no relationship to any real person or actual event.

First Edition

1 2 3 4 5 6 7 8 9 10

Library of Congress Cataloging-in-Publication Data

Weeks, Dolores.
The Friday Harbor murders / Dolores Weeks. — 1st ed.
p.   cm.
I. Title
PS3573.E325F7   1988
813'.54—dc19   88-16846
ISBN 0-396-09367-1

For Chuck and Sue
with love

My sincere thanks to Ellie Scott
and my friends
at the Women's
University Club, Seattle

1

Gale-force winds blew the rain in sheets against the house. The parched grass on the banks above the tidal pools soaked up some of it. The rest spilled over the rocks and ran like a river out to sea. From Goose Island, the cries of thousands of gulls floated to shore.

Dr. Scott Eason grabbed the mail off the front seat of the Jeep and raced to the door of his San Juan Island summer cabin. The black and white sheep dog, who'd been sitting beside him, splashed behind. Scott reached to the top of the beam inside the doorway, ran his fingers along the splintered edges of the wood until they rested on the nail.

No key! Damn! Should be there. Had he failed to put it back last visit? He dug into his pocket for the spare, finally found it, turned the key in the latch and shoved. The door didn't budge. Warped, he guessed. He put his shoulders behind it, shoved again. Shuddering, it gave way.

Inside, it was cold and damp. The house had been shut up all of April and May while Scott had been stuck in Seattle with a heavy surgical schedule, and it smelled musty and sour, as though it had been unlived in a much longer time.

Scott flipped the light switch. Nothing happened. "Power's out!" It wasn't an unusual occurrence here on the Cape where high winds rolled in from the Pacific with great regularity, knocking down power lines and putting stress on transformers. But today was Sunday, and he knew it would be tough getting the linemen out to repair the damage very quickly.

The dog roamed into the kitchen. Scott felt his way into the living room, guided by the luminous spray from the waves crashing against the rocks below his deck. Everything black except the frothy-covered seas. "Better get some light in here."

He deposited the mail on the big round table in front of the fireplace and went in search of the kerosene lamp. He fumbled around the stereo cabinet until he put his fingers on the metal base, removed the glass cover, and struck a match to the wick. A tiny flame slowly put a dim glow over the rooms. He looked around the living room, which opened into the kitchen. All appeared to be as he'd left it.

Outside, a giant white-capped roller broke over the corner of the deck, and a foaming gusher thundered into the air. The gale sent an echoing moan through the rafters. Scott thought about Erin, three thousand miles away. He'd resigned himself to Spencer's coming to foul up his vacation, but Erin delaying her return from the East brought a deep ache to his chest.

She was on a two-month job that had already stretched into three, decorating for the furniture markets in Highpoint, North Carolina. "Wonderful experience for an interior designer," she'd said. "Bob Finley recommended me."

"Finley?"

"He's the furniture rep here. I've known him for years."

But Scott hadn't believed she'd gone to get more decorating experience. Nor did he believe it was the reason for her staying longer than she'd contracted to stay. Now, he thought glumly, she's back there with no plans to return soon, and I'm here, and there's no ring or promise or anything to hold us together, and it's all my own stupid fault. One failure at marriage had made him gun-shy, and whatever block was lodged inside him, he couldn't bring himself to say the words he knew Erin wanted to hear.

2

A quick burst of wind shook the living-room shutters, and a branch of the big fir brushed the glass. Wind and surf whistled and rumbled in deafening concert with each other. Normally, storms on the Cape excited Scott. It was the best part of living on this wild corner of the island. But tonight it failed to rouse him.

Another gust blew a fountain of spray across the deck and washed down the big living-room windows. "Winds kicking up, Dandy." The dog wasn't paying much attention to the wind. He had his eyes on the empty dish on the kitchen floor.

"Cold in here," Scott observed, feeling the chill through his down jacket. "I'll get a fire going, and then we'll bring in the rest of the gear." Dandy settled down beside the refrigerator with a thud. "We'll get something to eat, too," Scott promised.

Scott was searching for newspapers in the wood box and barely heard the knock over the howling wind. Dandy heard and barked. Hope rising, Scott went to the door. Absurd notion, thinking he'd look down into Erin's sky-blue eyes, greet her with a big bear hug, feel the softness of her honey-blond hair against his cheek. He opened the door, but it wasn't Erin. Standing in her place was a skinny old man and a sopping-wet fluffy little dog.

"C'mon in, Al."

Al sort of blew in, sloshing water all over. His small brown eyes peered up at Scott from under a flopping rain hat, which dribbled water over the edges. It was Erin's grandfather, retired history professor Al Turner, buried in a yellow rain slicker with sleeves that hung inches over the ends of his bony fingers, and Chips, his small white terrier. Chips bounced around the room, shook puddles of water on the entry tile, and raced into the living room behind Dandy.

"Hey, settle down there," Al shouted after them. The dogs dropped on the rug beside the big windows and carried on a whining conversation. Al shrugged. "Power's out."

"I noticed."

Al lived by himself in the house across the road, and he and

Scott were friends as well as neighbors. The old man had his usual down-on-the-world look, but Scott was pleased to see him all the same. His humor, if you could call it that, hung on sarcasm, but he was alert and sprightly for seventy-five, a good companion in spite of the near forty years' difference in their ages.

"Come on in the living room, Al. I'm about to get things warmed up."

Al removed his hat and hung it, dripping, on the hall peg. "Highest tide in a hundred sixty-eight years. Could do some damage to your deck."

Scott checked the windometer on the cedar-paneled walls of his living room. The needle bounced perilously close to fifty knots. "A real southwester, but I'm well above the high-tide line. We should be all right."

Al sniffed disagreement, hung his jacket under the hat, and followed Scott into the living room. He stood by the stone fireplace wall where Scott was struggling to open the damper and blew on his hands. "Cold in here."

"Stuck." Scott grunted, shoving harder on the iron lever. It broke free, and a cloud of heavy, black soot fell from the flue. "There we are." He wadded up a newspaper, set it on the grate.

"Aren't you afraid of a downdraft in this wind?"

"Stack's on the west side. Wind goes right over it." Scott piled kindling on top of the papers and struck a match to it. Paper and sticks burst into flames, sucking up the chimney like a leaf in a wind tunnel.

"Mmpf," Al said, and sank into the big chair next to the hearth. "You haven't been up in a while."

"Lot of surgeries last month."

"You missed the big fire."

Scott nodded. He'd read about the fire at McKay Harbor that had taken the life of an Indian and twenty-five fishing boats, newly delivered to the Indians. "That was over two months ago."

The old man reflected. "Seems like a couple weeks. They thought it might be arson."

"Was it?"

"Never did find out."

McKay Harbor, on Lopez Island, was only a short fetch across the waters of Cattle Pass, and Scott imagined those flames had put a fire into the night sky that matched the Northern Lights. "You sure had a front-row seat."

Al nodded. "Lit up the pass for hours." Then, observing the pile of mail Scott had dropped on the table, he said, "You been stacking mail for two months?"

"No. Bulk of it gets forwarded to the house in Seattle. These are bills, mostly." There was no letter from Erin. He'd looked.

Scott pulled a log out of the wood box, set it on top of the flames. "I see the dig at American Camp is coming along nicely." The dig near the historical site of the American-British Pig War was an archeological project of the state college, and Al had been down on it from the start.

"Mmpf," Al said. "Bunch of fool kids shoveling dirt around, dropping their beer bottles and brown bags all over the landscape. It's a disgrace."

Students had been on the island for months now, dressed in jeans and sweats, digging in the yellow grasslands overlooking the cliffs above the strait, carving layers of sand and mud out of the rocky ground.

"Colleges must have money to burn." University waste was another of the old man's favorite gripes.

"I understand they found some interesting Indian artifacts, Al. A Tsimshian rattle, a hunting spear, both in excellent condition. The remains of an old Indian woman, and a good deal more."

"Mmpf. Don't know where you heard that. The Indians never permanently located here. They spent summers fishing and hunting, that's all. They're not going to find much."

The room heated up, in spite of the cold wind blowing outside. Scott fed both dogs, and Al leaned back against the cushions of the big chair, pulled out the old Alpine pipe from his shirt pocket, and lit it.

5

Scott reached for another log.

"Speaking of the dig," Al said, this time with a smirk, "I see our junior senator is coming on the island to dedicate the whole darned mess."

Scott dropped the log on the fire and stared at the old man. Spencer had written his visit was to be a vacation and strictly private. No politics, he'd promised.

"It was in the Friday Harbor newspaper. Anniversary of the Pig War." Al smiled cattily. "Thought *you* would've heard. According to the paper, Spencer Manning's staying right here with you."

Scott sat down on the hearth, feeling a little sick. He had plans for his vacation. A little sailing. Walking the beach with Dandy. A night or two fishing with the gillnetters. He had no plans to entertain a bunch of politicians. It was all to be much worse than he'd imagined.

Al drew on the pipe stem. "Didn't know the senator was a friend of yours."

Spencer, a friend? Acquaintance was a better word. "He's an old fraternity brother. Haven't seen him in nearly five years. He called two weeks ago, asked if he could come up to spend a quiet retreat for a few days."

"Quiet, huh? What he wants is publicity. Stands for reelection next year."

It fit. But how much publicity would Spencer get on a small island like San Juan, with one town — Friday Harbor — only a few short blocks long, total island population, including dogs, cats, and summer people, of not more than three thousand, and one small weekly newspaper? Certainly, the island's residents weren't what Scott would call political. Fact was, fishing, bicycling, and boating were of far greater interest to most islanders than a visiting senator.

"He's likely to be disappointed, if that's why he's coming."

The lamp flickered, and the long shadow of the poker stick played the shape of a tribal spear against the stone.

Al sucked on his pipe. "He's fence-mending, I expect. If it were

6

me, I'd give San Juan Island a wide berth. Fishermen are hopping mad at him."

Scott was a little surprised by this. He had close friends among the purse seiner and gillnetter operators who fished the island waters and hadn't heard Spencer's name come up even once. "What did Spencer do now?"

"You really have been gone awhile. It was his vote on the North Pacific Fishing treaty. Cut the salmon quota for the Americans in favor of the Japanese and the Russians. Hasn't won him any friends around here, I can tell you."

"Terrific!" Scott said unhappily.

Down the end of the hall, the bedroom door shook.

"Wind?"

Scott walked to the entry and looked down the hall. Dandy and Chips were scratching at the closed door. Scott called them back, and Al went on talking.

"You and the senator go back a long way, I take it."

"From grade school, although we were never very close. Spencer was a couple grades ahead of me and always running for something. When we finished college, he went on to law school. Shortly after that, he ran for the legislature. Then Congress. Rest is history."

The scratching started again. "Chips!" Al snapped. The noise stopped. "Don't see you two as a match."

"We more or less got thrown together my freshman year in college when we both hired on here as counselors at the Alderwood Camp."

Al's lips turned up in a smile.

"Don't laugh. Spencer was a strong swimmer, had a way with teenagers. Particularly the girls."

"Now, why doesn't that surprise me?" Al screwed up his nose. "Do you notice something smells bad in here?"

Scott drew a deep breath, caught the smell, more strongly now than when he'd first come in. "Wonder if a mouse died in the rafters."

7

Al sniffed again. "More likely a rat."

From the kitchen, the dogs began scuffling and growling, kicking up considerably more racket than usual for them. Scott started for the kitchen. Al followed.

"My God, what a stink!"

Scott quickly saw the cause—a badly decayed fish, which the dogs were busily tearing up and throwing around the floor.

"Don't eat that!" Al shouted, springing with Scott for the dogs.

They pulled them away and picked up the pieces of fish, wrapped them in newspaper. Scott deposited the package outside and mopped the floor.

"Where do you suppose they got it?"

"Don't know, but I think I'd better find out." Scott looked under the sink at the kitchen garbage sack. It was empty, just as he'd left it. He took the big flashlight from the laundry room and torched it down the hall. Al and the dogs followed close behind. The smell grew stronger with each stride, strongest when they reached the bedroom where the dogs had pushed open the door.

"I got a bad feeling," Al said.

Scott walked into the room first. The stench caused an uncomfortable wrench in his stomach. He aimed the torch at the bed. Nestled in the middle were three badly decayed salmon. Pinned to the pillow was a large piece of ruled notepaper blotted with fish blood.

"My God!" Al gasped.

Dandy and Chips started for the fish. Scott grabbed their collars and, holding his breath, bent over to read the words printed in bold letters on the bloodstained paper.

SENATOR SPENCER MANNING—REST IN PEACE!

2

Al covered his nose with his hand. "Who would play a mean trick like this?"

"Someone who doesn't like Spencer." Scott fought off a wave of nausea. "Whoever did it, I've got to get it out of here, and fast."

Al retrieved a roll of paper towels from the kitchen, and they cleaned up the mess, deposited the remains of the fish in the trash outside, put the note in the laundry room, dumped the bedspread in the sink to let it soak. Scott threw open the bedroom windows and let the gale blow through.

"Going to get wet in here."

"Got to get the smell out."

"How do you suppose they got in?" Al was clearly shaken by the idea that someone could have broken into the house only a few yards from his own front door.

Scott checked the windows on the water side. They were all locked tight, no broken glass or even a sign of forced entry. Then Scott remembered the key that had been missing by the front door. "They must've used my spare key."

"Who'd know about that?"

Scott shrugged.

"I should've kept a better watch."

"Don't be silly. You can't have eyes in the back of your head."

Al shook his head, still blaming himself, and Scott said, "Why don't I get out the Coleman and make us a cup of coffee?"

The old man brightened at the suggestion. "Darned power company. Ought to have the power back on by now. Oh, make mine tea, would you, Scottie?"

Scott started up the propane burners on the little camp stove, and Al speculated about the intruder. "I told you the fishermen were mad at Spencer."

It was, of course, what Scott was thinking. The commercial fishermen were edgy these days anyway with the dwindling salmon runs and the State Fishing Commission closures that were shortening the season more each year. Contributing to their troubles was the court ruling on an old Indian treaty that allotted half the catch to the Indians. This had caused open hostility between the Indian and non-Indian boats. Now, it appeared, Spencer's vote on the international treaty had put him squarely in the middle.

Scott and Al sat with their tea. "The more I think about it," Al said, "I'm sure it's only a prank. Delivering a message to the senator. Childish and mean, I grant you, but no irreparable damage has been done." Al even began to see humor in the situation.

To Scott, the kind of mind that could be driven to such antisocial behavior suggested frightening possibilities, but he said only, "Whoever did it wasted his energies. Spencer won't arrive until Saturday."

The wind rattled the front door, and the dogs began barking. Scott opened the door and looked into the lean face of Billy Leroux, owner of the Indian fishing boat, the *Billy Jean.* Billy was normally a cheerful man, but there was no smile on his face as he shivered on Scott's porch, his windbreaker soaked through so his bones showed.

"Hi, D-doc, saw the sm-smoke comin' out your stack."

"Billy! C'mon in." Scott took his jacket, hung it on the hall peg, and led him into the living room. Billy was still dripping water as he backed up against the fire and continued to shiver. Scott poured coffee into a mug, laced it with brandy, and stuck the mug in Billy's hand. He swallowed gratefully and, after a while, seemed to thaw out. He had the look of a man with a problem. "What brings you out on a night like this?" Scott asked.

"Things getting ugly," Billy said, running his words together. "Sammy mounted a twelve gauge on his bow yesterday."

Al jerked up in his chair. "The Indians are running with shotguns? Why do they want to do a darned fool thing like that? Want to start a shooting war?"

"Wouldn't have last year. This year, I dunno."

"What's different?" Scott said.

"Runs are worse. Not enough fish to go around. More boats coming in, crowding the regulars."

"You and Vic are getting along?" Vic Larson owned the hundred-foot purse seiner the *Nellie J* and was a friend of both Scott and Billy. Vic was also the recognized leader of the island fishermen.

Billy nodded and gulped the last swallow of coffee.

"What then?"

"This senator who's coming to stay with you—"

Scott and Al exchanged puzzled glances.

"Vic's organized all the boats. He's got this plan to blockade Friday Harbor when the senator comes in on the ferry."

Al grinned as he caught the idea. "And the fishing boats are going to stop the senator's ferry from docking."

"That's the idea."

Al thought it was funny, but Scott thought about dead fish and all those fishing boats, the big purse seiners, gillnetters, and bow pickers, tied together, forming a solid wedge across the opening to the harbor, and the ferry with Spencer standing on her decks waiting to land—Spencer, who'd never had much of a sense of humor. Would it make him even more resistant to the plight of the fishermen? And if Spencer lashed out at the fishermen, how would Vic and the others take that? Maybe there'd be more guns. Ugly, as Billy said. "I take it Vic is fixed on this idea?"

11

"You know Vic."

"Stubborn Norwegian," Al agreed.

Billy still looked troubled.

"That's not all of it?" Scott guessed.

Billy dug into his pants pocket and pulled out a wadded-up sheet of lined paper, thrust it into Scott's hand. Scott recognized the paper immediately as he unfolded it. Like the note on the bed, the words were printed in large capital letters. Al's smile faded swiftly as he read with Scott.

WE'RE THROUGH SCREWING AROUND. WE'RE GOING TO FIX THE SENATOR FOR GOOD!

"Where did you get this?" Scott said.

"I got it from Vic. He got it from this crab fisherman, Herm Bruner."

Scott stuck the note in his pocket, walked over to the fire, and began pushing the logs apart with the poker stick.

Al got the idea. "You go on. I'll stay with the fire."

Scott pulled his jacket off the hall peg and grabbed the blood-soaked piece of paper from the laundry room. "C'mon, Billy. We're going to see Vic."

Billy groaned. "Why did I know you were going to say that?"

Billy and Scott piled into the Jeep and drove the short distance to the creek.

Fish Creek, a small backwash on the backside of the Cape, opened up into Griffin Bay, looking north up San Juan Channel. It was sheltered from the west by Mount Finlayson, but caught the north winds straight on, and the low sand isthmus that separated it from Cattle Pass offered only slight protection from the squalls that kicked up off the strait to the south.

At the Fish Creek docks the pleasure boats tossed in the wind. At the north dock where the fishermen tied up, the smaller gill-netters and bow pickers strained at their lines, but Vic's purse seiner, anchored by three hundred tons of wood and steel, thumped only lightly against the pilings.

The *Nellie J* wasn't a palace as far as live-aboard facilities went.

It was a boat designed for fishing. But it had been Vic's home since his third divorce two years ago. "One piece of real estate the old lady can't touch," Vic had told Scott. It was as solid as an oceangoing tug. The drum and skiff covered the stern. Below-decks were the hold and the engine room. Forward were the flying bridge and the wheelhouse. Behind the wheelhouse was Vic's live-aboard cabin, which held a galley with wood stove and refriger-ator, bunk, and table. The bunk doubled as sofa. The table served as a desk. They were cramped quarters, but since Vic spent most of his time outside anyway it didn't appear to bother him.

They found Vic sprawled out on the bunk in his stocking feet and briefs, television blaring, two empty beer cans and a clipboard in front of him. The room was all steamed up and smelled of beer and cigarettes. Vic wasn't a big man, but he was muscular with powerful shoulders and arms. He had coal-black hair, shaved so short his leathered skin showed through, a leftover from his ser-vice days in the marines. He had dark eyes that turned black when he was angry. When Scott faced him with the note, his eyes flashed their anger on poor Billy.

"You shot your mouth off?"

Scott held the note in front of Vic's nose. "What do you know about this?"

"I've seen it. Herm Bruner found it tacked to my cabin door." He continued to glare at Billy.

"Who's this Bruner?"

"Crab fisherman from Alaska. Thought I told you about him. The Coast Guard confiscated his boat up in Bristol Bay, said he was crabbing outside international borders."

"Was he?"

"Probably. How could he help it the way the borders meander these days? Anyway, he's fighting it. Fat lot of good it'll do him. He blames the Fishing Commission and the new treaty. You know something, Doc? He's got a point. He's got a cool million tied up in that boat."

"He blames the senator, too," Billy said. "He's plenty pissed at him."

Throwing Billy another look, Vic continued. "Bruner tells me he wrote this fuckin' senator, but all he got back was a bunch of bullshit about sharing with the Russians."

"If they confiscated his boat, what's he doing down here?"

"Court costs were eating him up so he came down to work the season. Signed on to crew for Davey on the *Mollie O*."

"You think Bruner wrote the note?"

Vic shrugged. "I suppose he's mad enough."

"What about this blockade?"

Vic bristled. "Doc, I don't care if the senator is your friend, we're going to shut down Friday Harbor so tight, a seagull won't slip through. We're going to show those butts in Washington we mean business."

Scott saw the frustration in his friend's face and felt a soft pull at his chest. "It's not the blockade worrying me, Vic. It's the threat against the life of a United States senator."

Vic wiped beer froth from his chin and settled back on the bunk with an is-that-all look. "Aw, shit, Doc, that note doesn't mean anything. The boys got a little overheated. Nothin' more to it."

Scott pulled out his own note and handed it to Vic. He and Billy read it while Scott told them about the fish.

Vic frowned and began to pace barefooted around the cabin. "Dumb bastards. They'll screw up everything."

"We have to tell the sheriff," Scott said.

Vic read the note again and slowly nodded his head. He reached for his jeans off the bunk and started pulling them on. "Okay, I'll tell Leroy. But I'm not calling this deal off."

It was twenty minutes by car to Friday Harbor from the Cape through driving rain and over rut-puddled roads. Vic grumbled all the way about nosy Indians and people getting hysterical. Billy, wisely, said nothing.

The sheriff had a good deal to say. Leroy Bates was a widower in his mid-forties and, like Vic, something of a loner. He was also a fair-minded and normally soft-spoken man who took his job seriously, but without always giving the appearance of doing so.

Scott knew firsthand he wouldn't be rattled in a crisis. He also knew he was a cautious person who liked to avoid trouble before it happened.

Scott showed him the note and told him about the fish. Leroy immediately picked up the phone, tapped out his private numbers to the federal authorities in Seattle. He explained the situation, apparently not receiving fully satisfying answers. "Sure," he said, "we have security here, but we're not Seattle. We're a small island. We're underequipped and understaffed...." He said a lot more, which all amounted to the fact that he expected help. Apparently, he wasn't to get it. When he put the receiver down, he looked greatly displeased. He frowned at Vic across the desk. "How long you been sitting on this, Larson?"

"I haven't been sitting on it. Only got it this morning."

Leroy shoved his chair back and stood up, all six feet six of him. The thirty-eight hung smartly from his waist. "I could lock you up right now, and I've half a mind to."

Vic sprang to his feet, came up to about Leroy's chin. "What the hell for? I did just like the doc, here, told me to, didn't I? I brought you the fuckin' note."

"For conspiring to impede commerce."

Vic threw Scott and Billy a see-what-you-got-me-into look. "We're not impeding anything. We're just doing like the fuckin' Indians. We're protesting. Anyway, how did you hear about it?"

"Doesn't matter."

Billy piped in. "Vic's got a point, Sheriff. Indians demonstrated last summer. Nobody said a word."

Scott knew Leroy was basically on the side of the fishermen, as were most of the islanders. Scott also knew the sheriff had his own problems with city hall. "Leroy, isn't the harbor demonstration something that could be worked out with the commissioners?" Wasn't it better, he said, for the fishermen to vent their anger?

Vic lit a cigarette and listened while Scott pleaded his cause.

"How would it look for the state's junior senator if he appeared

15

to be denying the men their rights?" Scott said. "Face it, Leroy, you get more congestion here during the weekend of the Jazz Festival than you'd get from a two-hour boat-in."

Vic blew up a smoke cloud and nodded enthusiastic agreement.

Leroy frowned. "You're in charge?" he said, looking at Vic.

"Damn right."

"You can keep it under control?"

"Anybody doesn't do like I tell him will be picking his teeth out of his net."

Leroy let out a disgusted sigh. "Okay, Larson. I'll talk to the port commissioners. I'm not promising anything, but I'll try."

Vic's face said he wasn't happy with the indefiniteness of Leroy's pledge. Leroy returned to the problem of the threats. "Do you know who might have written these notes?"

"Don't have the foggiest."

"Doc?"

"I really don't."

Billy leaned forward. "There's a couple guys from up north been throwing their weight around. Tall guy with frizzy hair and his sidekick, short, heavyset, red hair. Both mean as they come."

"Have they got names?"

"Tall one's Todd. Don't know his last name. They call his partner Red. Red's the troublemaker."

"You know who he's talking about?" Leroy asked Vic.

Vic gave Billy a disgusted glance. "Todd Sweeney. His partner is Red Thompson. They come from around Bellingham. Operate the gillnetter *Judy Lynn*. They mouth off a little. Doesn't mean anything. They're throwing in with us on this blockade. Wouldn't do that if they'd written the notes, now would they?"

Leroy wrote down the names and then, looking at Vic, said, "I want a list of all the boats taking part in this deal."

"Why?"

"Doesn't matter why."

"C'mon, Vic, how else is the sheriff going to clear this with the port?"

16

Grudgingly, Vic agreed to bring the list.

Billy started squirming around again.

"Something else on your mind, Billy?"

Billy nodded. "Toughest one of the whole bunch is Herm Bruner."

"Bruner?"

"Guy who found the note. Buddies with Red, and he's got it in for the senator, real good." Billy told Leroy about Bruner's crab boat.

Leroy pushed his chair back. "Where can we find him?"

"Near the customs dock."

"C'mon," Leroy said, pulling his jacket off the coat tree beside him. "We're going to get it straight from the horse's mouth."

The wind blew rain into their faces as the four of them trudged cheerlessly down the long dock. It was slick underfoot, and Vic, leading the way, tripped once. He swore and continued on.

It was dark and quiet on the *Mollie O.* The rain drummed loudly on the metal spool. That and the wail of the wind were the only sounds on her decks. Vic shook his head. "He's not here. Probably over at the Drift-Inn with the boys."

"No — he's here," Billy said.

"How do *you* know?" Vic snapped.

"He's here most of the time. Got no place else to go."

Leroy banged on the cabin door. They waited. Nothing happened.

"I told you," Vic said irritably.

"He's probably asleep."

Leroy rapped again, this time with a heavier fist. The wind whistled through the rigging and brought another wave of rain. Scott pulled up his collar. It wasn't much use. They waited.

"Waste of time," Vic grumbled.

Leroy tried the door handle. It was unlocked. He opened the door and peered inside. Strong smells of whiskey poured out. "Dark as a cave in here."

17

Vic sighed impatiently. "There's a light on the starboard side that runs off shore power."

Beside Scott, Billy began to shift nervously. "Maybe Vic's right. Maybe we should come back later."

Vic grabbed Billy's arm. "What the hell's the matter with you, dancing around like a speared fish? This was your idea, remember?"

"It's cold out here," Billy muttered.

Leroy fumbled around, finally found the switch. Bright light illuminated the cabin and torched a trail onto the deck. "Oh, hell!" Leroy sighed. Then, "Doc, you better come in here."

Vic froze in the doorway. Scott looked at the floor where he was staring. Bare feet and legs clad in blue jeans were crumpled up against the bunk, and there was blood on the cabinets and the bunk, blood everywhere. He was lying face down, bare from the waist up. He was a big man, with rolls of fat around his waist and a thick neck. Behind him, Scott heard Billy gasp: "Bruner!"

Scott knelt beside Leroy and touched the bare skin. It was rigid. Herm Bruner was dead.

3

They rolled him over so he lay face up. Raw tissue and muscle bulged from a gaping hole in the crab fisherman's neck.

"Holy Mother!" Billy said, crossing himself.

"Looks like he was raked to death," Vic said.

Scott studied the jagged tears on the skin and nodded. "Cut the trachea, tore into the artery."

"Strangled?"

"Asphyxiated. He just stopped breathing." Then Scott spotted the wood handle sticking out from under the stove. He poked at it, slipped it out gently, careful not to grip the handle. On the other end was a sharp metal hook. Traces of tissue clung to it. "There's your rake." Whoever killed Bruner had gaffed him as though he were a fish.

Leroy nodded solemnly. "Caught him from behind from the looks of things. One quick thrust and it was all over." Leroy frowned at Vic. "You say Davey Olson owns this boat?"

Vic nodded. "He's off island. Won't be back for a couple days."

Leroy called his office on his two-way radio, and in minutes his deputies arrived and dusted the cabin for prints. The coroner followed to prepare the body for removal. Billy walked out on the deck for some air. Vic studied Bruner a minute and then signaled Scott with his eyes and started out behind Billy.

"If you need me . . ." Scott said to Leroy.

Leroy shook his head wearily. "Thanks, Doc. I'll be in touch." They left him huddled over the body with the coroner.

On the drive back to the creek, Billy did most of the talking, which wasn't like Billy, who was usually a better listener. Between his shivering and chattering, he sounded like a stuttering chipmunk. He wondered why anyone would kill Bruner, although only an hour ago he'd listed a number of reasons. Of one thing he was absolutely certain — it wasn't the Indians.

All this time, Scott waited for Vic to sound off, but Vic just smoked his cigarette and watched the raindrops slide down the window. Scott guessed he was wondering if Bruner's murder were somehow going to foul up his plans for the blockade. Scott had another concern of his own. Did Bruner's death have anything to do with Spencer's coming, and, if so, didn't Spencer have to be warned?

Calm seas and bright sun awakened Scott. The power was back on at the Cape, and if it hadn't been for the murder, everything would have appeared normal. Dandy ran to the beach, poked around the logs, and chased a crane into flight. He splashed through the incoming wavelets and returned to the grass mound just below the desk to shake himself dry. Scott placed the call to Washington, D.C. and reached Spencer's secretary.

Spencer had already left the nation's capital for Washington State, but threats were nothing new to the senator, the secretary said. "We get them all the time. Goes with the territory." He took the news of the murder with a disinterested "I see." Clearly, he didn't *see* how it affected Spencer.

"Where can I reach him?"

"He was staying at the family compound, but I think he's on the road just now, and I'm not sure where you can catch him."

Scott couldn't help smiling. The "family compound" was a small dairy farm north of Seattle, run by an elderly couple Spencer had hired to live there after his parents died. Since Spencer was an only child, he'd inherited the farm and used it as his legal residence. As far as Scott knew, he returned to it only when he was campaigning.

The secretary sighed impatience. "Didn't Cliff call you?"

"Who?"

"Cliff Wallace, the senator's advance man, takes care of these sorts of things. He's on the island right now. He was supposed to get in touch with you about a reception."

"What reception?" Scott said warily.

"Reception for the senator. It's customary on these visits. I thought you'd know. They said you were holding it at your house."

"Not my house! It's much too small."

"Uh-oh. I have another call coming in. Don't worry, Doctor. Cliff will contact you."

Scott barely put the phone down when Leroy walked in carrying the familiar valise with the fingerprinting apparatus. He wanted to take prints of the bedroom, he said, on the off chance there might be a connection between the threats and Bruner's murder.

Scott led him into the bedroom. "Things are a little wet in here."

"Can't get good prints when they've been washed down."

"Sorry. Did you try picking them off the notes?"

"Except for your prints, they're clean."

Scott pointed out if the writer of the notes hadn't left prints on the notepaper, it wasn't likely he would have left them around the house. This didn't deter Leroy. He sprayed graphite onto the counters and window frames, laid plastic tape over the surface, and lifted it off. He did this several times, making an incredible mess before he finally declared his job done and packed up to leave.

"Think we'd better security-proof your house," he said as he piled into his station wagon.

"What does that mean?"

"String a few wires."

Scott groaned. Holes in the walls, people crawling about. Why couldn't Spencer just stay in Seattle and forget the Pig War? An oceangoing tug chugged through Cattle Pass pulling a log boom. Leroy's eyes followed its passage. Even if Spencer's staff wasn't taking the threats seriously, Scott knew the sheriff was. "Do you see a connection here to Bruner's murder?"

Leroy rubbed the steering wheel of his car thoughtfully. "No. 'Course, number of nuts running loose, you can't be sure."

Discouraged, after Leroy left, Scott dropped in on Al. Dandy and Chips greeted each other with their usual whining and growling and then settled in the living room where Al's long-haired cat, Archimedes, sat on a pile of Al's papers and watched them with distrusting eyes. Al was preparing breakfast. He'd heard about Bruner on the morning news.

Scott rested his elbows on the kitchen counter and told him about his conversation with Spencer's secretary.

Al removed a bacon strip from the fry pan, dripped grease on the stove top, and set the bacon, still sizzling, on a piece of paper towel. "You're not going ahead with this stupid reception idea?"

"Definitely not!"

Al nodded approval. "Gotta draw the line somewhere." He cracked an egg into the pan, reached for another. "Had breakfast?"

21

Scott inhaled the sweet aroma of the bacon and confessed he hadn't.

"Sit down," Al ordered.

They ate and talked about Bruner and the fishing problems. Al screwed up his nose at Leroy's security measures. Then he got on the subject of Spencer's voting record. "Shows a deplorable ignorance of history."

Scott didn't care to look at his voting record, particularly now he was to be a houseguest for a week.

"His wife comes from money, I understand. No children."

"I've never met her."

Al soaked up egg yolk with his toast. "You say the senator's something of a lady killer?"

Scott nodded, remembering that summer at camp and Spencer continually recruiting Scott and the other counselors to fill in for him while he kept his dates in town. "Say, Al, whatever happened to Holly Clayborn? Did she leave the island?"

Al stuck a piece of bacon into his mouth and blinked surprise. "Thought you knew. She overdosed on sleeping pills about ten years ago, shortly after her husband died."

Holly dead. It was one of those disturbing pieces of news. Scott remembered a shy, pretty little girl, eager to please, soft-spoken, who'd had such a crush on Spencer that summer.

"Sad case," Al said. "She married Barry Dickson. You remember him? Big, good-natured kid who played lineman for the island football team?"

Scott nodded. "He crewed on one of the crab boats. Drowned in a storm off Alaska."

"That's the one. He and Holly married right out of high school. Hurry-up wedding, I heard." Al poured coffee into Scott's mug. "What made you suddenly think of her?"

Scott bit off a piece of toast. "No reason."

In the living room, books and papers littered the floor where Al had been working on his history of the islands. Scott stepped over a copy of *Northwest Passages* and found a clear spot on the sofa to sit with his coffee.

Out on the water, a large ketch cut a threadlike trail through Cattle Pass. Peaceful waters. High tide. Scott thought about his own little sloop, the *Picaroon,* gathering grass on her hull in Fish Creek.

Al walked over to the north window, which looked out toward Scott's house, and peeked through his blinds. "Uh-oh, you've got company."

Two women were stepping out of a small white Honda on the driveway.

Al grinned. "The Republicans have landed. Madelyn Ellis and Nancy Gristad. Guess what they're after?"

"Can't imagine," Scott said sourly.

"They see your car. Uh-huh. They know you're around some-where. Regular bloodhounds, those two. Uh-huh. Here they come."

"Damn!" Scott sighed.

Nancy Gristad, the wife of an island dairy farmer, was a pleas-ant woman of about forty. Blond and slightly plump, she had a chipmunk smile and was inclined to nervous chatter. Her name was always popping up in the Friday Harbor newspaper for being involved in the hospital guild, church charities, and precinct-level politics.

Madelyn Ellis was a tall, slender woman, neatly groomed with pale lips, black hair, and a distant manner. She was the wife of Dick Ellis, one of the attorneys in town. She'd been a camp coun-selor that summer with Spencer, and as Scott recalled, another of his old flames. Her marriage to Ellis, an island boy, had come the following year. Like Nancy, Madelyn was deeply involved in pol-itics and, unlike Nancy, definitely not a follower.

Scott had had only occasional contact with the two over the years, primarily because he'd never been interested in the island's social life, of which Madelyn was a distinct part, and because he'd always had a strong aversion to politics.

Al opened the door and waved the women in.

"Thought we'd find you here," Nancy said cheerfully.

Madelyn walked up behind her, clutching a large flat purse under her arm. She reminded Scott of one of the trial lawyers who seemed to come around far too often in medicine these days, unsmiling, singleminded, taking their depositions.

"Do you think this patient's injuries are reasonable for the accident described, Doctor?"

"Yes."

"Can you prove it?"

Scott's stomach twitched.

They sat in the living room, and Madelyn got right to the point. "Our women's club wants to hold a reception for Senator Manning, and the senator's secretary said we should clear it with you. Did Cliff Wallace call you?"

"He might have tried. I haven't been home."

"I suppose we jumped the gun slightly, but Cliff thought we could work with you on this. The senator and I are such very old friends, you see. Naturally, I wouldn't want to interfere with your plans —"

"You're not at all. I have no plans."

"I was referring to the reception. I hoped you wouldn't mind sharing Spencer."

"I have no plans for a reception."

Madelyn's brown eyes widened. "Then you haven't talked to the secretary?"

"I talked to him, but it's like I told him, I'm not set up for anything like that."

Madelyn moved to the window and looked across the road at Scott's house. "Of course, your home *is* small. How many rooms do you have?"

"Kitchen, living room, bedroom, den that doubles as a bedroom, bunk room that doubles as a laundry room. Get a dozen people in there and you have a crowd."

"A nice-sized deck," Nancy observed, pausing by the desk to stroke Archimedes. The cat accepted her attentions with a yawn.

24

"We might have to move things out, bring in some lawn furniture for the deck," Madelyn said.

"It's perfect! At least we don't have to paper the house." They laughed at what was clearly their own private joke.

"I hate to disappoint you," Scott said, "but you'll have to find another spot."

Nancy drew in her breath and the two women looked at each other. Their faces said they'd been totally unprepared for rejection.

Scott felt a twinge of guilt. "Surely you can find a suitable hall in Friday Harbor."

"Quite out of the question," Madelyn said. "Too many security problems."

It was a point Scott hadn't considered.

"You wouldn't have to lift a finger, Doctor," Nancy pleaded. "Madelyn and I will do all the work."

Madelyn nodded vigorously, and then said to Nancy, "We can get Amy North to cater."

Scott felt cornered. "I'll have to think about it."

Nancy brightened.

"Good," Madelyn said, as though it were settled.

Scott started to say something, decided against it. He'd settle it later with Cliff Wallace.

Al poured coffee, and they hung around, cementing their plans and going on about the senator's splendid work in Washington, all of which Al took in with an "Is that so?" or "I didn't know that." His sarcasm went right by them, and finally, they left, in very high spirits.

Madelyn paused on her way to her car. "Oh, Doctor, I forgot to mention that my son, Robbie, will probably stop in to see you. He's the senator's page, you see, and he thought he might be of some help while Spencer is here."

"I'll look forward to meeting him," Scott said.

Al choked on his pipe.

Later in the afternoon, Scott stopped at Fish Creek to see how

25

the *Picaroon* had survived the storm. Just seeing his small sailboat in her slip, her mast rising above the canvas tops of the small run-abouts on each side of her, filled him with longing. What a joke it would be on Spencer and the rest of them if he set sail right now and didn't return until the whole silly business was over.

Scott retied the boat's lines and returned home just as the postal carrier was leaving his drive. With a resigned sigh, he removed a stack of envelopes from his box, and this time it *was* there. A letter from Erin.

Out on the pass a number of small pleasure boats bobbed around in the cross chop. The poles hung over their transoms as they fished the deep tidal pools between the reefs. With the sun beating down on his bare back, Scott sat, legs hanging over the sides of the deck, and read her letter.

Dear Scottie,

I imagine this will find you back on the island getting some space from patients and schedules. I thought about the *Picaroon* yesterday, imagined sailing in Griffin Bay in a stiff wind, getting a good soaking down. I could almost feel that cool, salt spray sting my cheeks. Nothing like it here. We're miles from water. It's hot and muggy, and not much relief in sight.

We put two rooms together today, which is some kind of record. I found a wonderful oil painting of a New England fishing village to hang over an oak commode in the dining room. The painting reminded me of that day in Campbell River and the curious little boutique off the quay.

Scott smiled, remembering. Off the rocks a seal stuck its head out of a patch of kelp. Dandy raced to the beach, and the seal ducked under the water again.

Bob Finley, the man who hired me, was just made senior vice president here. Pretty amazing for someone so young. He's only thirty. He took me to dinner at a typically North Carolinian restaurant last night, a pleasant colonial place. Good food, too. Bob says the company is pleased with my work, and he talked about the possibility of my going on to the Atlanta and Dallas markets. Would mean an extra month or two, but it pays well and would be marvelous experience. What do you think?

I imagine you're having fun fishing, sailing, and just being lazy. Hope you have a fantastic vacation. Have to close now. Early day tomorrow. Give Dandy a hug. I miss you.

Love, Erin

Bob Finley again? Wasn't he the one Scott had met at the markets in Seattle with Erin? Tall—maybe Scott's own height, six feet two—not as muscular as Scott, perhaps, but a long way from puny. Dark-brown hair. (Scott's was blond.) Deep voice. Intelligent. Agreeable sort. Scott had liked him, in spite of himself.

Out on the water the small boats rocked and pitched in the swiftly moving currents of the pass—outboards, inboards, open cockpits and covered. Scott counted fifteen. A yell went up from one of the boats. A big salmon pulled free of its hook, left a disappointed fisherman staring unhappily at the cut end of line.

All at once Scott felt an emptiness that would hardly be filled by a visit from Spencer Manning.

Later, when the sun left the deck in shadows, Scott wrote to Erin. He told her about Spencer's visit and Madelyn and Nancy, about Vic's plans and the dig, left out the murder and the threats. No point in upsetting her.

"The *Picaroon*'s in tiptop shape and ready for a good wind," he wrote. "Will miss your competent hand." He wanted to say

27

"Come home, my love, and we'll sail north into Desolation Sound, wander back around Bird Cove, trace the long arms north to the quiet lagoons, and forget Spencer and medicine and the furniture markets." Instead, he wrote:

> Your success comes as no surprise. Know it will all come out a smashing triumph. Next thing you know they'll want to make you president of the company. Write soon.
>
> Love, Scott

4

Scott didn't sleep well, thinking about Bruner lying in the *Mollie O*'s doghouse, his throat cut open, and then, for no reason he understood, about bright red flames eating up the evening sky over Cattle Pass. Questions floated through his head all night. Was Bruner's murder an isolated incident or was there a connection to Spencer? Spencer would arrive in only a few days. Scott had to know.

Early in the morning, Scott dropped in on Leroy to see how his investigations were going.

"Bruner's wife is flying in this afternoon to claim the body." Leroy sighed heavily, and Scott knew this was one of the parts to his job the big man had no taste for. "Ran the gaff hook for prints."

"Turn up anything?"

He shook his head. "Wiped clean. Talked to those two fishermen from Bellingham."

"Did they help?"

"Todd Sweeney's a total blank. Red Thompson claims the Indians wrote the notes."

"Do you believe that?"

"No."

"What's this Red like?"

"Surly. Vulgar." Thumbs tucked into his gun belt, Leroy stood by the window which faced the street. The island double-decker tour bus was just poking its bright-red nose around the corner, headed for Roche Harbor on the other side of the island. "Something eating at that bird. When I find out what it is, maybe we'll know more."

Scott left Leroy's office and drove to the marina. Near the customs ramp in the harbor the masts of the commercial fishing fleet rose like light poles over the cabins of the pleasure cruisers. There was a sharp smell of salt in the air, and the docks were washed clean from the rains. The big purse seiners and the smaller gill-netters rafted side by side, masts held secure by heavy wire stays. Pulleys and lines draped off their booms. Their nets were rolled up on the big reels like fat spindles of yarn, and the decks were spotless, everything battened down in readiness. The word was the men were to get a night out, and there was a lot of happy bantering back and forth.

Scott sensed the excitement as he walked down the dock.

"Hey, Doc, wanta catch a few silvers?"

"Wish I could," Scott said.

On the second pier, in sharp contrast to the upbeat mood of the others, a glum-faced Davey Olson, wearing his familiar Mariners baseball cap, paced in front of the *Mollie O* as he watched the sheriff's men working over his boat. Two deputies crawled around the small bow picker, poking and probing, spraying for prints.

"Leroy's going to tie me up the whole damn day," Davey complained, "and we're supposed to get a night out, maybe tomorrow."

Scott nodded sympathetically. There were nets to get ready, prep work to do, and the delay might make him miss the run. Davey could be out thousands of dollars, money needed for the

29

upkeep of the boat, for shares to the crew. With the shortened season, none of the men could afford to sit out even one night of their allotted days. Davey was understandably upset.

"Bruner?" he said, staring cheerlessly at a foaming spot on the water where a fish had just jumped. "I wish I'd never set eyes on the son of a bitch. I felt sorry for him about his boat, but he was trouble from day one, always running out when there was work to do, meetings all the time."

"Who was he meeting with?"

"Dunno. Maybe his lawyer."

"Can you think of anyone who had it in for him? Who'd want to kill him?"

Davey shrugged. "He didn't make many friends. Had a mad against the world, that guy."

"I was thinking of special enemies."

On the *Mollie O*, one of the deputies knocked over a water bucket. It made a big racket as it rolled across the deck.

"Hey, watch it," Davey shouted. Then, "What were you saying, Doc?"

"Did Bruner have anyone in particular he disliked?"

"Senator Manning. He hated his guts."

"Anyone else?"

"Umm."

"Hey, Olson, will you unroll your net?" a deputy called out.

"Why?"

"You want *we* should do it for you?"

Davey threw his hands up in disgust. "Oh, hell. Sorry, Doc. I gotta go. Wish I could be more help."

Scott stopped by a couple more boats. He knew most of the fishermen on a first-name basis and had no trouble getting them to talk.

"Bruner? Except for those two characters from Bellingham, never saw him with anyone."

Scott soon saw Leroy's problem. Herm Bruner was a stranger to San Juan Island. No one knew much about him. He had died a violent death, but the struggle had taken place during the storm when everyone was holed up in their boats. No one saw Bruner go out of his cabin or anyone else go in. The only noise anyone would have heard was the howl of the wind.

On his way home, Scott stopped by the dig. This was where Spencer would make his public appearance, and he wanted to see it up close. He parked the car in the nearby park grounds and walked over to the slopes where the students were busily working to repair the problems brought on by the heavy rains. Above the site, wind-twisted firs framed the crest of Mount Finlayson. Below were the shimmering blue waters of Griffin Bay.

Scott studied the steplike layers of clay and dirt that covered the hillside to the tide flats and observed that in some places the trenches were over six feet deep so a person could be lost in the shadows of their clifflike overhangs. The students had draped plastic sheeting over the cuts. They'd pumped water from the deeper holes and were now filling in with sand.

"Pretty heavy rains. We had to stop the flow of water or it would've all slumped in and destroyed the promising sites." The youthful voice belonged to a pleasant-faced young man in his early twenties with rosy cheeks, clear blue eyes, and an even smile. He was standing ankle-high in mud in one of the cuts, dressed in shorts and wearing a sweatband around the pale wisps of his hair. "I know you," he said to Scott. "You're Dr. Eason, Senator Manning's friend. I'm Robbie Ellis. The senator's page." He rubbed his palms dry on his shorts and gripped Scott's hand firmly.

"Your mother mentioned you. I understand you've also been helping the senator's advance man, Cliff Wallace."

"I've done a little footwork for him."

"What kind of work does he do?"

"Publicity, mostly. Makes sure there's a good turnout for the senator's appearances."

"You mean people don't automatically flock to see the senator?"

"You have to build crowds," Robbie explained.

A girl with straight, sun-bleached yellow hair working nearby

31

watched curiously. She was dressed in a halter top, jeans, and hiking boots, and there was something vaguely familiar about her. Scott smiled at her, and she turned quickly away.

"Incidentally," Robbie was saying, "I understand the senator's staying with you while he's on the island. Could you use an extra pair of hands?"

"What about your work here?"

"I'm just filling in."

"How are you as a cook?"

Robbie's smile shrank. "Not much experience there. Did my mom tell you I was jib man in the Swiftsure race last season?"

Scott laughed. "So you're a sailor, are you? Drop by. Maybe we can work something out."

Robbie grinned appreciatively.

That afternoon, Scott met Cliff Wallace. He appeared on Scott's deck in a starched white shirt—no tie—and slacks and introduced himself. He'd been staying at a hotel in town, driving around the island in a rented car. He was in his late thirties and, like Spencer, sparely built. He bore a striking resemblance to Spencer even to a certain singleminded manner, but unlike Spencer, he had black hair, brown eyes, and heavy-rimmed glases that had a tendency to fall forward on his nose. He was continually adjusting them.

He sat stiffly erect on the deck rail and glanced often at his watch. "I flew in a week ago. Meant to call sooner. Been tied up with the mayor and the Pig War committee."

"Can I get you a cup of coffee?"

"No, thanks. Have to be back in Friday Harbor. Meeting with the commissioners."

A Great Egret, croaking noisily, floated down to the water's edge. It gathered in its white wings and settled on the log poking out of the big driftwood pile. Beside Scott, Dandy stirred.

"Nice place you have here," Cliff said.

"Thanks."

"Did Madelyn Ellis talk to you about the reception?"

32

"She talked about having one," Scott said warily.

"Ah. Then it's settled."

"It's not settled at all, if you're thinking of having it here."

Cliff's face showed a mix of surprise and disappointment. Scott guessed he wasn't used to disappointment.

"As I told Madelyn, my home is much too small."

Cliff glanced around the rooms. "No problem. These affairs are better when people are mashed together. Makes a small crowd look big."

"But I don't want to mash people together in my house," Scott said, beginning to be annoyed. Using his home for politics was not part of his arrangement with Spencer. "I don't want to have a reception — period."

Cliff frowned. "Didn't Madelyn tell you we had security problems in town?"

"She mentioned it, but I can't see how it would be any better here."

Cliff pushed his glasses back on his nose. "Logistics, Doctor. Here, there's only one way in and one way out."

"You're forgetting the water."

Cliff ignored the point. "Town just isn't a viable option. I know it's an inconvenience, but the women will do all the work. We were counting on you, you know."

Scott felt trapped. "I see," he said, unable to think of any argument that wouldn't sound unreasonable. He would let the women do it all, he thought vengefully. He finally agreed on those terms. Cliff hung around a few minutes longer, telling Scott how well Spencer had done.

"Did you know he's been mentioned for vice president?"

Scott couldn't hide his surprise. "No. I hadn't heard."

"He's a driver." Cliff smiled, and Scott wondered if in some strange way the publicity man saw himself as an extension of Spencer. Before he left he stood by his car with some last-minute instructions. "If the media people call about the threats on the senator's life, refer them to me."

33

Scott stared at him. "You're letting it get in the news?"

"Of course."

"But didn't the sheriff tell you he wanted it kept quiet?"

Cliff shoved his glasses back on his nose. "You don't understand politics, Doctor. Publicity is the name of the game."

As Cliff predicted, the threats made the evening news. Leroy called Scott, irritated about the leak. Scott told him what Cliff had said, and Leroy sputtered something about a population that had gone brain dead and rang off.

The following morning the weather turned foul again. Word slipped out about Vic's planned blockade. Scott ran into an angry Cliff coming out of the sheriff's office. Water fogging his glasses, Cliff stood in the rain and complained to Scott about Vic's plans. He'd been trying to persuade Leroy to call the whole thing off and his face said he'd not been successful. "Who *is* this Vic Larson anyway? He sure has a lot of clout around here."

"He's a top-rate fisherman and a close friend of mine," Scott said in an irritated voice.

Cliff backed right down. "I'm sure he's sincere, but his timing couldn't be worse. The senator comes in on the noon ferry, precisely when the fishermen plan to bottle up the harbor."

That was, of course, the whole idea. "He could fly in."

Cliff shook his head vigorously. "Bad politics. Would look like he was ducking the issue."

And he'd miss the publicity, which, as Cliff had pointed out himself, was what it was all about.

5

For Scott, the rest of the day was a wash-out. It was too wild for sailing or snorkeling or much of anything except observing the fuss everyone was making over Spencer's visit. To make matters worse, Madelyn, Nancy, and the members of their women's club arrived on his doorstep and began work on his house.

"Tidying up for your company," Nancy said with a toothy grin.

Scott looked around the living room—magazines and newspapers on the tables, Dandy's rawhide bone on the carpet in front of the sofa, a few unwashed mugs sitting around, his boat-model tools on the television tray by the south window where he'd left them. Not bad. Only take a few minutes to pick it all up. This was Wednesday. Spencer wasn't due until Saturday. "That's nice," he said, "but I can manage."

Nancy wasn't listening. She was studying the stereo cabinet with a frown. "I don't quite know what to do with those records sitting on top."

"Leave them as they are."

She shifted back and forth on her heels and looked to Madelyn for support. Madelyn didn't shrink from the job. "Cliff tells me the senator plans a press conference here as soon as he arrives. We thought you'd want the house in order."

35

Behind her, two helpers picked up Scott's old leather chair from its position of importance in front of the fireplace and headed down the hall with it.

"Hey, where are they taking my chair?"

Madelyn smiled tolerantly. "It takes up too much room. We didn't think you'd mind our leaving it in the bedroom. Of course, if you object . . ."

Scott threw his hands up in the air. "Do what you want. I'll get out of your way so you can finish tearing things apart." Feeling as childish as Madelyn's glance said he was, Scott took Dandy and left the women to their work.

In town, he found Vic tied up in a different kind of preparation for Spencer's coming. Scott spotted his friend sitting at a table in the Drift-Inn tavern with some of the other fishermen. They were charting the harbor and selecting skippers for the lead boats in the blockade. It was Vic, the marine sergeant in charge, tackling each problem as though he were mounting an assault on Pork Chop Hill.

"Need men with guts," Vic confided to Scott after the others left. They would scatter the big purse seiners around to protect the smaller gillnetters and cushion them with the skiffs. "That way no smart ass can ram the line."

They were all working so hard, and, unless Spencer had changed remarkably, Scott feared it wouldn't accomplish much. "I hope you won't be disappointed," he said.

Vic looked up from his charts, the dark eyes amused. "Aw, hell, Doc, if it just scares the piss out of the little bastard, it'll be worth it."

The weather didn't improve. The following day Scott went about his own business of preparing for houseguests. He stocked the house with food, split logs for the fire, cut the brush behind the house, and performed the odds and ends essential for the dreaded visit. He dug out his scuba gear and checked it out. Spencer had said he wanted to dive. Scott was pleased the equipment was all in top shape. He stopped at the creek, changed the oil on the *Picaroon*'s engine and then lubricated the outboard on the runabout.

The next night, with Spencer due on the late-morning ferry, the fishermen motored in from all over the islands to tie up in Friday Harbor. Lines of them rafted together, swinging at anchor in the wind and rain all across the bay. They rowed ashore in their skiffs and congregated in the taverns around town.

Scott and Dandy were walking up Spring Street with a new downrigger, a device used by sports fishermen to sink their lines deeper. He'd purchased the downrigger at the marina to replace one he'd banged up. Someone shouted, "Hey, Doc, c'mon, have a beer." It was Vic, rain dripping off his yellow slicker, standing in front of the Drift-Inn tavern. Loud country rock and boisterous laughter drifted from the open doorway behind him.

The tavern was jammed and smelled strongly of beer, smoke, and wet gear. The men were in high spirits and with the music and the yelling, it was deafening in the room. All Vic's crew was there—Swede, the pole man; Mack, the cook; and Georgie, the skiffman. Across the room at a table near the wall, Robbie Ellis was entertaining the girl from the dig. The girl looked underage. Robbie waved, and Scott waved back.

Scott set the downrigger under the counter and settled on a bar stool beside Vic. Dandy shook water all over the place and slumped to the floor at their feet.

Swede poked a boot at the downrigger under Scott's foot. "Hey, Doc, whatcha gonna do with that cute little black ball? Bomb the fish outa the water?"

This brought a horselaugh from Vic. The commercial fishermen looked on most of the sports fishermen's gadgets pretty much as a cowboy viewed a mechanical horse.

"Let me guess," Swede said. "The visiting senator?"

"Ha!" Mack said. "That guy couldn't hit the floor with his foot."

They were having so much fun joking and laughing about

Spencer and the downrigger they weren't paying attention to the other end of the bar. When a voice shouted, "Fuck off, you asshole!" they all stopped talking almost at once.

The voice belonged to the square-built man with carrot-top hair and brown-freckled arms.

"Red Thompson," Vic said, frowning.

Beside Red, Billy rested his elbows on the bar. He looked very much under the weather.

"Herm Bruner had a big mouth and so do you," Billy said to Red in a thick voice.

Vic moaned. "There's going to be trouble. Billy's had a snootful."

Red's jaw clamped down tight, and where there'd been anger, there was now rage. "Listen, you fuckin' Indian, it's all in his log."

Billy raised himself off the bar, looking like a peanut squaring off against a tank. "You're full of shit."

Someone threw a punch. Scott and Vic started for Billy, expecting to see him flat on his back. When they reached him, Billy was standing over Red. Billy's fingers were folded into brown fists, and Red was sitting on the floor, blood drooling from his mouth, looking very surprised.

Swede grabbed Billy by the arm and began steering him toward the door. "I'm taking him back to his boat."

Vic nodded agreement. "Yeah, get him outa here before we get *big* trouble."

Billy had a half-wild look as Swede and Mack dragged him out, Red flinging four-letter words after him.

Vic frowned. "Bad blood between those two."

"What's it all about?" Scott asked.

Georgie, who liked to gossip, told Scott that Billy had called Bruner a butcher, and since Red and Bruner had been friends, Red didn't take it well. Red said Bruner wasn't to blame and that he'd written it all down in his log.

"Blame for what?" Scott said.

Georgie shrugged. "Dunno. But did you see the way Billy flattened him?"

"Maybe we should talk to Red. Find out what he knows."

"You won't get anything out of that mussel-head tonight. He's three sheets to the wind," Vic said.

It was close to eleven when Scott finally left the tavern. The streets were still wet, but it had quit raining, and from the number of stars flickering through the clouds, it looked like the weather was going to improve. Scott struck a path for the sheriff's office.

Leroy was still there, going through a stack of paper, and grumbling about it. Scott told him what Red had said. "Maybe nothing in it, but I thought you should know."

Leroy nodded. "The ship's log. Yeah, we looked at it. Nothing there except where they fished, how much they caught, tidal conditions, winds, currents — the usual stuff."

Scott was impressed with Leroy's thoroughness, but disappointed. He'd had the feeling the log might be important.

"Any trouble at the tavern tonight?" Leroy asked.

Scott thought about Red sitting on the floor, licking blood off his lips, hate strong on his face as he watched Billy being dragged out. "Pretty normal for a Friday night, I think," Scott said.

Leroy flashed a knowing smile. "Hope it stays that way."

6

A circus atmosphere hung over Friday Harbor when Scott and Dandy arrived. The sun shone brightly. Ice cream and T-shirt vendors wandered at the foot of Spring Street, and from the bandstand outside Sunshine Alley, the Island Jazz played "Sweet Georgia Brown." Scott got a whiff of popcorn when a small boy ran past sprinkling kernels all over the sidewalk in front of the Sweet Tooth Salon.

All along the shore a solid mass of people collected. Pleasure boats ran in and out of the harbor much as usual for summer, but more were coming in than going out. Dozens had already rafted together outside the floating dock breakwater where they could get a closer view.

Television crews from the three major Seattle stations had set up their cameras at the end of the customs dock, and one of the news teams from Bellingham was circling the bay in a helicopter. Scott observed the steep slope of the dock ramps with a frown. Low tide would make it shoal at the edges of the bay. But Vic would have planned for that.

Scott found a ledge at the end of the gas dock a short distance from the ferry pilings, less than fifty feet from where the fishermen would line up, and Dandy and he sat down to wait. It was hot, not a whiff of wind, and all the way east to Shaw Island the seas were quiet. Slimy green seaweed floated on the exposed surfaces of the pilings and the whole bay smelled strongly of fish.

By the ferry hut, Cliff, Madelyn, Nancy, and the welcoming committee crowded around the rail, looking expectantly across the harbor. The ferry would arrive momentarily. Scott suspected Madelyn and her friends would have a long wait before Spencer put his foot on shore.

"Can you see anything up there?" Leroy squinted at Scott from under the brim of his Stetson.

"Good view. Come on up."

Grumbling about the town being overrun and no place to stand, Leroy climbed up beside Dandy, banged his thirty-eight against the piling, and complained some more.

"I thought you'd be in the patrol boat," Scott said loudly enough to be heard over the sound of the Island Jazz.

"That's Harold's job," Leroy shouted back. Clearly, Leroy wanted to be closer to the ferry landing and Spencer. Leroy removed his hat and mopped his forehead. "Hot." He looked impatiently at his watch. "*Kaleetan*'s overdue. Damn ferry system. Never do run those things on time."

Scott caught the tension in Leroy's voice, and for the first time

40

realized how much stress the blockade must be placing on him and his men. With Bruner's murder, it was surprising he'd let Vic go ahead with it.

"Anything new on Bruner?"

Leroy shook his head.

"Or the notes?"

Leroy looked disgusted. "Getting information out of the fishermen is like trying to pry open a clam with a toothpick."

Scott nodded. If the fishermen knew one of their own had written the threatening notes, they'd keep it to themselves.

A siren pierced the air. The Island Jazz stopped in the middle of a note, and three short bursts from a ship's horn followed. From the shore, a dog howled. Dandy whined restlessly.

"Must be Vic."

From both sides of the opening by Upright Head the first boats nosed around the bend. The *Nellie J* led from the north reef. The *January,* an Alaskan seiner skippered by a friend of Vic's, led from the south by the bell buoy. One by one they followed—Davey Olson's *Mollie O*, just released from Leroy's investigations, Billy's gillnetter, the *Billy Jean,* Red and Todd's *Judy Lynn,* and the others. They edged toward the breakwater, the big purse seiners with their sturdy skiffs resting on their sterns, the gillnetters and the bow pickers, with their cutter bows and big drums, nets rolled around them, empty. They broke a white path across the harbor opening, closing a half circle around the breakwater. The rumble of their engines mingled eerily with the cries of the gulls, like a fleet of landing barges coming ashore onto a quiet beach.

The skippers stood behind their wheels, square-shouldered. The crews stationed themselves on the decks, proud men pushed beyond the limits of their understanding.

Vic was at the wheel of the *Nellie J,* and Scott knew he'd be barking orders over his ship radio to the other boats. "C'mon, Davey, swing your bow in closer. You're letting her drift . . . Pull in, *Judy Lynn,* you're running off course. . . ."

They fashioned a giant arc and, like a marine drill team, low-

41

ered their skiffs. They dropped them smartly beside the big boats, scattered them systematically through the line, tied them securely, so boat linked to boat, seiner, skiff, bow picker, gillnetter, skiff. Scott lost count at eighty. The ships closed ranks, edged together so bow pulpits hung over stern rails, so close a rope wouldn't slip between.

The sun beat down brightly on their decks, and Scott felt a lump in his throat as he watched them perform in near-perfect synchrony. The water rolled under their keels and shot up from their stern rails in glistening white plumes, and Scott ached to join them. He thought about all the boats that had gone broke in the past year and those in arrears to start this season and found himself hoping that maybe a glimmer of enlightenment would strike Spencer and those who made policy. Scott thought about Spencer and how he'd be pumping hands with the local politicians and how they'd all be underfoot for a whole week. Discouragement settled in.

The bells and horns on a fishing boat play a distinctive sound, loud enough to warn another boat in the fog, to signal a greeting across a short fetch of water, to express joy at a full catch, or to sound an alarm. The deep blast cut the air, loud and urgent. It did not come from the fishing boats. It was the *Kaleetan* ferry, and she was five minutes out, just coming up on the light at Upright Head.

It was the moment everyone had waited for when the fishing boats, forming their impenetrable wedge, would repel the ferry, send her back into San Juan Channel to wait out the protest or, perhaps the ultimate insult for Spencer, to return to the other islands without depositing her famous passenger.

She let out another blast, and Leroy drew a deep breath. "She should be turning in another minute."

"How far will she come into the harbor?"

"Can't come too far. Should make her turn before she passes the first channel marker."

Scott saw the marker, just off the University Experimental Lab toward the north shore. To her port, the water would be shoal. Middle of the harbor, below the surface was a dangerous reef. With the low tide, the ferry would have to stay in her channel.

On signal, the fishing boats shut down their engines. They sat, rocking gently, tied together, bow to stern, skiffs rafting between and alongside, anchored at the extreme end of the bay by the shallower-keeled boats. Scott watched with Leroy, waiting for the ferry to circle and head out. She approached the docks to the north by the lab.

Leroy stroked the handle of his gun.

The ferry passed her first marker and didn't stop.

"What the hell?" Leroy said, annoyed.

Scott thought, She'll turn now. Logic would have it so. Logic lost. The *Kaleetan* continued on course.

"What's he doing? He knows about the blockade."

The *Kaleetan*'s horn exploded three more times, and the ferry headed slowly toward the ferry landing and the center of the fishermen's line.

Leroy dropped from his perch and landed on the gas dock. He whipped his radio from his belt and barked into it. "Harold, tell that damn ferry captain to back up and do it now!"

There was an answering rush of static and Harold saying "On my way."

Below them, the patrol boat turned on its outboard and ran the short distance to the breakwater. Overhead, Channel 12's helicopter swept over the water. Clearly, the media people sensed the *Kaleetan*'s moves weren't in the script.

The *Kaleetan* continued to head right for Vic and the *Nellie J*, and Scott knew Vic wouldn't budge. Perhaps the captain sensed it, too. The ferry veered slightly so that instead of pointing squarely at Vic's hundred-foot purse seiner, she headed toward the smaller, more vulnerable boats—Davey Olson's bow picker, the *Mollie O*, and Todd and Red's *Judy Lynn*. Both boats were under thirty feet and weighed considerably less than thirty tons. The *Mollie* was an open boat with a tiny cabin far forward. The *Judy* was a fiberglass job. If hit, she'd be crushed like an eggshell.

43

The *Kaleetan's* captain let out another blast on her horn and steered for the *Mollie*, all four hundred feet and three thousand tons aimed at the little bow picker. It was like taking on an ant with an elephant gun.

It wasn't usual for a captain of the state's ferry system to push the limits of prudence so far, and Scott wondered if he were under pressure from Spencer or some state official. Maybe he was rankled by the delay and merely sought his own solution to the problem. The only trouble with this kind of game was that if the captain hoped to intimidate Vic and his men, he'd badly miscalculated.

"If someone doesn't back down now, the ferry's going to turn the *Mollie* into kindling," Scott said, seriously alarmed.

Leroy continued to shout into his radio, trying to reach the ferry's captain. Scott imagined the airwaves must be jammed with Vic radioing his men to hold fast and the *Kaleetan* ordering the fishing boats to move or suffer the consequences. The ferry released another warning blast. This time Vic answered. Three quick bursts. Each boat in the line took it up, one, then another, then in unison until the whole harbor rumbled with it. The *Mollie* didn't budge.

Bells clanged frantically on the *Kaleetan*. Maybe it was becoming clear to the captain that the fishermen weren't going to back down, and if he stayed on his present course, he'd strike the *Mollie* midships and smash her into a thousand pieces. The great diesel engine chugged and clanked, heaved and creaked as it rammed into reverse and slowed its forward momentum. Enormous white waves gushed up around the bow and swamped the *Mollie's* gunwhales. Slowly, still rattling its warning orders to the engineer, the *Kaleetan* crept back. The fishermen let loose with sirens and horns and a cheer went up along the shore.

Vic raised his arm in a victory salute, and something in the water caught Scott's eyes. It was so swift and unexpected, few noticed. The *Judy Lynn* separated from the other boats, leaving a wide hole in the line. She headed out behind the *Kaleetan,* and the

44

boy beside Scott tending the gas dock speculated she was going after the ferry to even the score. Scott remembered the wild look on Red's face when he'd threatened Billy. But what could he do to the big ferry unless he ran with missiles on his bow?

On the *Mollie O,* Davey was staring at the freed end of line from his stern where he'd tied onto the *Judy Lynn*'s bow. The *Judy Lynn* was running in an aimless fashion around the bay.

"Why's he leaving the others?" Leroy wondered.

The water behind the *Judy* churned into white and blue rolls, forming a long, frothy V-shaped trail. Suddenly her engine quit, and the stern plume went flat.

Scott saw Red's partner, Todd, shoot out of the wheelhouse and run to the stern. Todd began tugging frantically at the line that dangled off the stern rail.

"What's he doing?" Leroy said.

Todd pulled and strained, pulled again, and finally the boom started up, slowly, as though something were weighting it down. Todd kept pulling until the shackled end of the line broke the water's surface.

Beside Scott, Leroy drew in his breath sharply. "My God!"

Hanging from the end of the *Judy Lynn*'s boom line was Red Thompson. In the early days of sail a punishment for insubordination was looping lines around an offender's feet, dropping him off the bow or the side rails, and dragging him face down in the water under the keel until he drowned or survived to repent. Red hadn't been keel-hauled. He'd been dragged like a fish, but not by his feet. He'd been pulled by his neck in a noose made from the shackled end of the rope, and the way his head swung almost free of his neck and his legs dangled limply under him, there wasn't much question, Red Thompson was dead.

7

The blockade broke up in confusion. Scott left Dandy in the Jeep and went with Leroy to the customs pier where they had towed the *Judy Lynn*. Uncovered, lying out on the dock, Red looked as though he'd been molded in paraffin. His eyes were sunk deep in his face. There were gaping tears in his throat, much like those on Bruner's except there was no blood due to the chill of the water. His head was set off at a rakish angle, broken at the back of the neck.

The reporters crowded around with cameras and tape recorders and viewed him as a fisherman might a dead fish. "Homicide, Sheriff?"

Leroy stared back at them and didn't answer. It was hardly likely Red would've put that rope around his own neck. No one would choose such a horrible death.

Leroy's deputies backed the reporters up the dock to give Leroy and Scott room to deal with Red. Leroy removed his Stetson and mopped his brow. It must've been over ninety on the dock, and with the cameramen aiming their cameras at him, he looked harassed.

"Died of strangulation, I guess," Leroy said.

Scott examined the thin strands of hair matted to Red's scalp.

A nasty contusion between the ear and the right temple was just the right location for a death blow. "Might have been struck here before he was thrown into the water."

Leroy nodded. "Hit him and looped the line around his neck. Then shoved him overboard."

"No one noticed the line being dragged with the wake from all the boats."

"Cover him up and get him out of here," Leroy barked to his deputy, Harold Cane.

"What do I do with his partner?" Harold said. "Wanta lock him up?"

"Where is he?"

Harold pointed to the stern of the *Judy Lynn* where Todd stood, the twisted coils of his hair sticking out in every direction. He was still staring at the cut end of the line that had dragged Red.

"Did he confess to it?"

"Nope. Keeps blaming the Indians."

Scott felt a jab of alarm.

Aboard the *Judy Lynn,* Leroy faced Todd. "Do you know who killed him?"

Todd scratched at the wild curls of his hair and said nothing.

"What were you doing while Red was being strangled by your line?"

Todd stared at a spot on the water where the sun laid a shimmering patch of white light and continued to say nothing.

"Were you and your partner getting along?"

This snapped him out of his trance. "Don't try to pin this on me. Red told me to take the wheel when we started. I been there the whole time."

"Who tied the lines if you were in the wheelhouse the whole time?"

Todd went back to staring again.

Out by the bell buoy the *Kaleetan* edged back into the harbor, weaving a slow path between the departing fishing boats. Scott figured she'd be another ten minutes. He decided to postpone leaving for the ferry landing a little longer to hear what Todd had to say.

But Leroy got no more out of the frizzy-haired fisherman. Davey Olson from the *Mollie O* cleared up the business over the lines. "I tied the bow line. Never did see Red. Billy tied the stern. We figured Red had bugged out 'cause as soon as we got near the breakwater there wasn't anyone on the *Judy*'s decks to take those lines, and she was about to ram Billy's stern. Me and Billy jumped over and fastened her down. Good thing we did, too, 'cause she was bouncing all over the place, could've done some real damage to Billy's boat."

Scott got another one of those uncomfortable feelings. "Where was Todd while you were doing all this?"

Davey shook his head in disgust. "Stoned, like always. Dumb bastard didn't know where he was. Can't figure how he got as far as the breakwater. I told Vic days ago not to depend on those two."

"Were they fighting with the Indians?" Leroy asked.

Davey shrugged. "Red was always fighting with someone."

The ferry slid past the breakwater. Some of the reporters broke through the deputies' line on the customs dock and began questioning Todd. "Who do you think killed your partner?"

"It was the Indian."

Across the way, the ferry landed. Scott struck out for the ferry hut, wondering fearfully which Indian Todd had in mind.

8

Spencer Manning, in jeans and a bright blue and white sports shirt, was just walking off the loading ramp when Scott reached the landing. At his side was an attractive, dark-haired woman in a red blouse and white shirt. Crowds of foot passengers coming off the ferry pressed around them, but Spencer had that aura of a celebrity that put him distinctly apart.

He hadn't changed much, thinner, perhaps, but still youthful, energy-charged. His ash-blond hair was thinning slightly, but there was the same ever-present smile, the friendly gathering in of hands and arms, the tenor voice.

Clearly unaware of the events on the *Judy Lynn,* he walked into the crowd, greeting people cheerfully. Halfway down the ramp he paused to talk into the television recorders, and someone told him about the homicide. Foot passengers brushed past, and Spencer stood there, no smile now, only shock on his boyish face.

From the back of the car line, a traveler honked impatiently. Then a shiny white Continental rolled off the ramp behind them, and Cliff guided Spencer toward it. Scott chose this moment to step in.

"Spence?"

Spencer spun around. "Scottie!" He grabbed Scott's hand and pressed it tightly, too tightly. "Good to see you, boy. Good to see you."

Up close, he was shockingly frail, and there was a fleshiness around his eyes that made Scott wonder if he'd been ill.

"Good to see you, too," Scott said.

Almost absently, Spencer touched the arm of the woman beside him. "You haven't met my wife. Gwen, this is Scottie."

She had a magnetic smile and flashing dark eyes. "Doctor," she said, offering her hand. "I've heard so much about you."

Her hand was smooth and soft, and she let it linger in his a moment. "I'm happy to meet you," he said.

"What's this about a murder?" Spencer asked anxiously.

"One of the fishermen. Tell you all about it at the house."

"Hey, Scottie, Cliff asked some reporters and friends out for a few minutes. Short press conference. Hope you don't mind."

Scott shrugged. "No problem."

Madelyn took over at the house, made coffee and herded the media around. While they all mingled in the living room, Spencer and Scott huddled in the study. When Scott finished telling him

49

all he knew, Spencer said he hoped he wouldn't be hurt by the fallout.

"Publicity?" Scott said in disbelief. "You're worried about publicity when two men have been murdered and there's threats on your life?"

He looked surprised. "But the murders have nothing to do with me. As for the threats, my driver's a bodyguard. He can handle any problems that come up."

"Does he look after your wife, as well?"

"Why would anyone want to hurt Gwen?"

"Maybe to get at you. Look, the kind of person who writes threatening notes isn't what you'd call normal. More than likely, he, or she, is a psychopath. Psychopaths can be extremely dangerous, and I don't think you should take it lightly."

Spencer chuckled. "Same old Scottie. Always the worrier."

Scott didn't smile.

"You think it's one of the fishermen writing these poison pens, do you?"

"Quite honestly, I don't know. They're good men, and they work hard, but they're having tough times. With the shutdowns many of them are barely able to make the payments on their boats. They have a legitimate beef, Spence. You really ought to hear them out."

"Hey, Scottie, I can't get involved in this thing. It's a political minefield. We've got a committee of the Congress studying the problem. They'll come up with something." He thumped Scott's shoulder fraternally. "Hey, boy, how about this great weather. Can we get in some sailing and diving, do you suppose? Maybe even a little fishing?"

In a cheerful mood, Spencer returned to the living room to join Madelyn and her husband and the media people.

Scott sought out Spencer's security guard, Jacob Long. Jacob—Jake, as he liked to be called—was in the kitchen drinking coffee when Scott found him. Jake, a black, was a big man, taller than Scott by three inches, with massive shoulders and chest and a soft-spoken manner. Scott liked him instantly.

He was dressed in a pale-gray sports jacket and charcoal slacks and looked a combination of Wall Street broker and noseguard for the L. A. Raiders. Actually, he was a Secret Service man, temporarily assigned to Spencer. It was a position, Scott gathered, he didn't like much. Clearly, he hadn't been fully informed about the problems on the island.

"It always helps to know what you're up against," he said. He'd been studying the security at the house. "I don't see any problems from the road. That's easy enough to track." Across Cattle Pass, the ice-blue waters twisted and stirred up whitecaps. He studied the small boats fishing in front of the house. "It's the water side I worry about."

Jake definitely understood the problem. Scott left him, confident if anything went wrong, the big man would know what to do.

In the living room, Spencer was engaged in a serious discussion with Madelyn's husband, Dick. On the deck, Gwen chatted quietly with Cliff. It was the most animated Scott had seen Cliff, and from the heightened color in his face, it was clear the man who didn't appear to warm up to people easily warmed up to Spencer's wife.

"I see you're enjoying the view," Scott said.

"Yes. It's lovely here," Gwen agreed.

A tern dove into the waves below them, leaving a gleaming swirl of foam on the water's surface. Cliff adjusted his glasses for a better look. "Very nice," he said, squinting into the sun. "I wonder, Doctor, could you squeeze in another boarder?"

"If you don't mind sharing the bunk room with Jake?"

Cliff laughed. "Jake snores."

"Poor boy," Gwen teased.

Cliff grinned at her. "The bunk room will be great." He glanced at his watch. "Uh-oh! Gotta get things moving for the press conference. See you later."

Gwen sighed after him. "Poor Cliff. Sometimes I think Spencer works him much too hard."

"He seems to like his job."

She nodded. "He was a reporter for the *Washington Post* when Spencer met him. He's a brilliant young man. Princeton. Columbia. Spencer snapped him right up. I wonder, though, if he's wasting himself in this job."

"Probably good experience."

"At least the pay's good."

"And the perks?"

This brought a knowing smile to her lips. "Oh, yes. Spencer has opened up some nice investments for his friends." She winked. "But you know all about that."

He smiled back, not telling her he didn't know, that he'd never wanted to be involved in Spencer's business deals. "Is Cliff married?"

"He was. She ran off with a stockbroker."

Scott felt a sudden bond with the publicity man.

"Spencer tells me your wife died."

He nodded. "Two years ago." He was going to tell her they'd been separated before that, but decided it would only raise unwelcome questions.

"I'm so sorry," she said. She laid her hand on his arm, the gentle instinctive gesture of one who touches as a way of communicating, and Scott felt a little pleasure tug at his chest. He was beginning to understand the change that took place in Cliff when he was around Gwen. She was the kind of woman men wanted to please.

"Your home is perfect," she said, "and it's so wonderful to be here, to be away—away from things."

He guessed she was going to say "Away from politics," but with the dedication next week and the presence of the island's political figures in Scott's living room, it wouldn't have been true. Scott imagined politics followed Gwen Manning wherever she went. Suddenly he felt sorry for Spencer and his wife—so little privacy in their lives. Scott, who cherished his, couldn't imagine a world without it.

"Was this to be a vacation for you?"

There was definitely a sadness in her smile, and he guessed she hadn't been entirely privy to Spencer's plans. "I'm sure it will be once Spencer is finished with his political obligations." She sat on the deck bench overlooking the rocks above the water's edge. Dandy, who'd been on the beach chasing a flock of terns, bounced up the stairs and went right over to her. "Hi, there," Gwen said.

Dandy responded by licking her face, a sure sign of his approval. She laughed and mussed up the thick curls of the dog's hair and asked about the islands and Scott's life as a surgeon. She was a good listener and laughed readily. She reminded him much of Erin, not quite as lighthearted, and a trifle sarcastic on occasion, which Erin wasn't at all, but generally, a vital, happy person.

They talked about skiing and sailing, which she enjoyed, although Spencer had little time for such pursuits, she said. "Did your wife like to sail?"

"She was afraid of the water." But Erin was a good sailor. "How would you and Spencer like to go for a sail tomorrow?" he said, surprised the idea excited him when only minutes ago, talking to Spencer, he'd looked on it as a chore.

"I'd love to." She touched him again. Her soft fingers resting on his bare arm caused another tremor. Warning signals went up. She was, he reminded himself, Spencer's wife. Then he wondered if Cliff had any trouble remembering that, too.

A curious quiet enveloped the house when Madelyn and Dick Ellis and the media people finally left. Like an actor offstage after the final curtain, Spencer collapsed in the big chair, the one Scott had moved back to the living room in defiance of Madelyn.

He looked totally drained of the energy that only moments ago seemed to charge through him like bolts from a high transformer. He removed his shoes and rested his stocking feet on the coffee table next to a bouquet of carnations and azaleas Madelyn had set there. He flexed a big toe and studied it thoughtfully. "Good to unwind."

Gwen sank onto the sofa and nodded agreement. Cliff and Jake had tactfully taken up residence on the deck where they stood at opposite ends, gazing at the waves breaking over the rocks.

"What a thoroughly pleasant spot," Gwen said with a long sigh.

"Are we on for a sail tomorrow then?" Scott said.

Spencer perked up. "And a dive?"

"If you like. How about it, Gwen?"

Gwen screwed up her nose. "Scuba diving?"

Spencer gave his wife a stage smile. "If you'd rather golf, I don't mind. Scottie and I have some catching up to do. You might be bored."

"We *could* do the diving some other time," Scott said in an annoyed voice.

Spencer frowned at the suggestion, and Gwen said, "He's right, Scott. I'd be bored."

Spencer buried himself in a copy of the San Juan Island newspaper and didn't look up.

Scott got a fire going and then put on a tape. While the strains of a Mozart violin concerto played soothingly through the house, they all found their solitary interests. Cliff remained on the deck gazing at the water. The tide was changing, and the waves were throwing up some nice white-frothed gushers onto the rocks.

Scott sat on the window seat in the corner and worked on his boat model. Gwen and Jake sat on the sofa reading. Spencer got up a couple of times to pick a different newspaper from the stack and then returned to the chair. For several moments there was general contentment in the room.

Scott was tying the rigging on a flying jib when Spencer got up and, newspaper clutched in his hand, sought out Cliff on the deck. They walked to the beach, huddled together, talking intently. Spencer was gone several minutes. When he returned, he no longer had the paper, and there was that distressed look Scott had seen on his face in the unguarded moment at the ferry landing. Spencer walked back to the bedroom and shut himself in.

A moment later, Cliff burst in from the deck, retrieved his car keys from the kitchen counter where he'd left them, and strode out to his rented car, muttering something about going into town for the senator. Shortly after, his car rumbled out the drive. Jake and Gwen observed it all with mild interest and returned to their reading.

"Something wrong?" Scott asked.

"The polls," Gwen said with a knowing smile. "Spencer feels he isn't getting enough favorable publicity."

"Too bad," Scott said, trying to identify with Spencer's problem but having trouble doing so.

Gwen laughed. "Don't worry. It's never any different."

In a few minutes Spencer returned and stood in front of the fire. He seemed to have worked through whatever it was that had bothered him, but when Scott offered him a glass of wine, he said, "Make it a bourbon and water, will you, Scottie, and easy on the water?"

Within the hour, Cliff returned, carrying a copy of the *Seattle Times* weekend edition, which he promptly handed over to Spencer.

Gwen and Scott started to prepare dinner. They were working together in a comradely fashion, everyone in a state of peace again, when a knock on the door drew Dandy from his spot by the refrigerator. He loped, barking, into the hall.

Jake, who'd been in the living room quietly reading a book, sprang from his chair and followed Scott to the door. Scott opened it, and there was Al, who looked back at them with a bewildered face.

"Scottie," he said hesitantly, staring at big Jake, who hadn't drawn his gun but looked about to.

"Hi, Al, come on in." Scott introduced him to Jake.

"It's a pleasure, Professor," Jake said.

"How do you do," Al said, continuing to regard the big man with suspicion.

Scott introduced the others and Al just stood there, looking worried.

"Something wrong?"

Al nodded. "It's Billy. Leroy just arrested him for Red's murder. I thought maybe he could use our help."

9

It was late, and the media had come and gone by the time Al and Scott reached the sheriff's office. Scott still smarted from Spencer's unsolicited request to be left out of it.

"I'd like to help, you know that, Scottie. But the election's coming up this fall. I can't afford to get involved."

"I don't remember asking you," Scott said.

"Politicians," Al muttered in disgust as he and Scott drove to town.

In Leroy's office, Vic pounded an angry fist on Leroy's desk. "Billy wouldn't hurt a fly."

Vic had been delivering his views on Billy's arrest for some time before Al and Scott arrived, and, clearly, Leroy was weary of it. "I have to hold him, and that's that," Leroy said.

"Why?" Scott asked.

Leroy looked up from his chair where he'd been stretched out with his feet on the desk and sighed heavily. "For one thing, witnesses saw Billy strike Red. For another, they heard him threaten to kill Red."

"Just liquor talk," Vic said.

"And there was another altercation a week ago with Red and Bruner at the fish buyer's barge. Buyer says Billy threatened to shoot both of them." Leroy dropped his feet to the floor. He had the intent look he was known for on occasion. "Now they're both dead."

It didn't sound like Billy.

"Where's the motivation?" Al said.

"How do you feel about ten thousand dollars?"

"What do you mean?"

"That's the amount that was stolen from Red's bunk."

"Who says it was stolen?" Vic snapped. "That doper Todd?"

"What has any of this to do with Billy?" Scott said, confused.

"We found ten thousand dollars in Billy's cabin in fifty-dollar bills. The money stolen from Red was in fifties."

"Proves nothing," Vic said.

"According to Billy's bank," Leroy continued, glowering at Vic, "Billy's been in arrears on his boat payments."

"Him and a thousand others."

Al leaned across Leroy's desk. "Sheriff, all these men deal in cash with their fish sales, isn't that right? There's nothing unusual about Billy having cash. The amount is just a coincidence."

Vic nodded. "Billy had a good catch last week."

Leroy turned on Vic again. "Then why can't he come up with a single receipt for his sales?"

"I'm sure there's a reasonable explanation," Scott said.

Leroy studied the three of them with sympathetic eyes. "I'm as sorry about this as you are, but until I find a good reason not to, I *have* to hold Billy."

Leroy was a fair man and level-headed, not the kind to arrest anyone without cause. Knowing this heightened Scott's concern. The evidence against Billy had to be substantial. "Leroy, you say witnesses heard Billy threaten Red. But did anyone see him around when Red might have been murdered?"

Leroy nodded. "That's the tough part. Billy's boat was tied next to Red's all night long. Plenty of opportunity. Then, in the blockade, Billy ran alongside Red. More opportunity."

"I planned it that way," Vic grunted.

"Uh-huh, and did you plan for Billy to tie the *Judy Lynn*'s lines to the skiff? Would've been pretty hard for Billy not to have seen Red dragging from that stern line when he did that, don't you think?"

It was a damning point Scott had thought of himself. "What does Billy say?"

"He claims he didn't see a thing."

"Can we talk to him?"

"Anytime you like."

In the small detention room where the sheriff had locked him, Billy paced restlessly. The windows on his concrete cell were barred, but there was a tightly woven carpet on the floor, a couple of chairs with vinyl seat pads, a bunk, a water closet, and a sink. It was far from uncomfortable. But for Billy, a man who made his living at sea, it was a cage.

Billy smiled when he saw them, but as soon as they settled in around him, his face sagged again with that look of abandonment. "I didn't do it," he said.

"We know that," Scott said.

"Fuckin' idiots," Vic said, throwing blame indiscriminately.

"Don't worry," Al said. "They can't keep you here. There's such a thing as *habeas corpus ad subjiciendum*."

Billy stopped pacing and leaned against the screen-barred window. "Habe-what?"

"It means holding someone without due process. It means we're going to get you out of here."

"Damn right!" Vic lit a cigarette and handed it to Billy, lit another for himself.

There was a glimmer of interest on Billy's dark face as he sucked on the cigarette.

"We'll need your help," Scott said. "You have to tell us everything you know."

A stream of light from the setting sun shone through the heavy mesh and caught the tired lines on Billy's face. "Told Leroy all I know—and here I am."

"When did you last see Red?"

"This morning. On his boat. About a half hour before we shoved off, he poked his head out of his cabin and yelled at Todd to pick up some cigarettes. Todd started down the dock, and Red ducked back inside, said something to someone, and that's the last time I saw him."

58

"Wait a minute," Scott said. "Said something to whom? Was there someone in that cabin with him?"

"I thought so. Todd says not."

"But you heard voices?"

"Heard Red's voice. I figured he wasn't talking to himself."

"The fish buyer said you'd been fighting with Red and Bruner, that you threatened both of them."

"They pissed me off."

Scott waited for further explanation, but he gave none. "You hit Red in the tavern last night," he reminded him gently.

"I don't remember it, but I'm sure it happened. Do some dumb things when I'm drinking."

"Leroy says you had a lot of cash on your boat."

Billy nodded glumly.

"Where did you get it?"

"I—I found it."

Vic's mouth gaped. "You what?"

"It's the truth. Found it in my bunk. Didn't tell the sheriff. Knew he'd never believe me. Looks like no one else will, either." He dropped onto his bunk and buried his head in his hands.

"You have no idea where the money came from?"

He shook his head vigorously. "First I thought I'd forgot it, you know, that I'd put it there after my last catch and got drinking. I was plenty glad to find it with the bank breathing down my neck. But I been thinking, and I know I'd never forget ten thousand bucks. I don't know where it came from. All I know is I didn't steal it." Billy's brown eyes watered. "How am I going to explain this to Helen and the boys?"

"Do you have a lawyer?"

"Never had need of one."

"We'll find one," Scott said.

"Lawyers don't come cheap."

"You let us worry about that," Vic said.

They left him staring bleakly at the bare walls of his cell.

"It doesn't look good," Al whispered.

59

Vic nodded. "That's not the worst of it. Leroy's thinking of charging him with Bruner's murder, too."

It struck somewhere in Scott's subconscious — Billy's nervousness the night they'd gone aboard the *Mollie O* to see Bruner, almost as though he knew they'd find the crab fisherman dead. Billy was hiding something. Al was right. Scott didn't see how it could look much worse.

That night Scott wrote a letter to Erin. She'd always liked Billy, and he knew she'd want to hear about his troubles. He told her about the blockade and the rest.

> The only way I can think to help Billy is to find out who actually killed Red and Bruner. As usual, the fishermen aren't talking. But someone knows something, so I guess Vic and I will just have to dig it out.
>
> It would be much easier without houseguests,

Scott wrote. He told her about Spencer's arrival and the people Spencer had brought with him.

> You'd like Gwen. In many ways she reminds me of you. I don't think she likes being in the public eye, but Spencer is what he is, and I don't think he gives her needs much consideration. We're going sailing and scuba diving tomorrow. Would be a nice break if it weren't for this business with Billy. Probably just as well you're not around this summer. What with Billy in this trouble and a crazy running loose, North Carolina sounds like a good place to be. . . .

10

Scott slept poorly, worrying about Billy, and by morning he was ready to escape on the *Picaroon*. But Spencer begged off on the sail to work out some political problems that kept him and Cliff on the phone and in discussions most of the day.

There wasn't much Scott could do for Billy on a Sunday and, irritated to be on someone else's schedule, he dropped in on Al, spent the afternoon helping the old man stack firewood, and complained about Spencer.

Al nodded understanding. "Houseguests are like dead fish. After two days, they stink."

The following morning, Scott rose early, loaded the air tanks for the dive into the Jeep, and drove into town. After conferring with Billy, he helped Vic settle on an attorney in Dick Ellis's firm, a trial lawyer named Brett Barnett. Barnett, a silver-haired man in his early fifties who had probing blue eyes and a quick grasp of things, promised he'd have Billy out of jail before lunch.

Vic dug into his pocket and pulled out a wad of hundred-dollar bills. He counted out thirty and slapped them down on the desk in front of the lawyer. "You tell me when you need more, but get the job done."

To Scott's raised eyebrow, Vic said, "Aw, hell, Doc. Billy hasn't got a pot to piss in. You know that."

Outside the attorney's office, Vic said he was going to start talking to the fishermen. "Somebody knows something he isn't telling."

After he left Vic, Scott stopped at the Underwater Shop to verify the tanks were full of compressed air for the dive. Everything checked. He rented two spares, and he and Dandy drove directly to Fish Creek to prepare the *Picaroon* for sail. He would get back to Billy's problems later in the day.

It was only nine-thirty when he reached the creek, and it was already hot. The sun had dried the dew on the docks, and the aroma of dried pine needles mixed pleasantly with the smell of fish and drying wood. The *Picaroon* sat quietly in her slip. All across the creek and into Griffin Bay the water shimmered a brilliant blue. Except for a small boat motoring north around Seal Rock, nothing moved in the whole bay.

Scott paused a moment on the dock to admire his little sloop, the clean lines, the double-ended hull — a lifeboat conversion — the sail, neatly covered by her canvas. Up close, he inspected the planked hull along her waterlines. As expected, after several months of limited use, there was grass growing on her bottom and a few barnacles crusting under the stern. Ought to be hauled for a scraping.

He climbed into the well, opened the hatch. Smelled musty. He pushed the skylight up and allowed the air to blow through. He turned the engine over. The Grey hummed, all cylinders working. Scott nodded satisfaction. She was fit and ready for sail.

He thought about Erin and running in the *Picaroon* through wild seas, letting the wind take them where it would. He wanted to jump right in, set a course up San Juan Channel, all the way past Bedwell into the Canadian Gulf Islands, pick a lazy path through the sheltered arms and inlets where other boats seldom ventured, put distance from everything. If only Erin was here and there was no Spencer and Billy wasn't in the mess he was in. He was, he knew, looking for an escape.

"How about it, Dandy?"

The dog's bark echoed his own eagerness to be on their way. Scott moistened his finger and held it up to test for wind. Nothing. The telltales on the mast hung limp. The windometer was as still as a rock in the sun. "Won't be much of a sail," he told the dog regretfully.

He returned to the house to pick up his passengers and walked into the middle of a disagreement between Cliff and Spencer. Disagreements with Spencer were not arguments in the normal sense. Smiling continually, Spencer made statements such as "I'm sure you did your best" or "I understand all that, Cliff, but I don't think I would have done it that way," far worse, Scott thought, than simply airing the grievance and getting it over with.

"I did the best I could," Cliff said, "but if it's not good enough . . ."

"Now don't get sensitive." Spencer patted Cliff's back.

Cliff's face pinked. He shoved his glasses back on his nose and said nothing. Spencer chipped at him some more, and, looking disgusted, Gwen walked out of the room.

Cliff had packed his gear into the Jeep, planning on going along as topside man, but it was pretty clear Spencer wanted him to work on publicity so he stayed behind.

Scott suggested asking Robbie to go in his place. "He's done a lot of sailing, and I think he's eager to go."

"Three's enough," Spencer said. "I'm not in the mood to baby-sit today."

Weather changed swiftly in the islands. In the short time it took Scott to return to the boat, a soft breeze had come up and rippled the waters of the creek. The telltales fluttered from the mast in a northerly direction, which meant the wind, such as it was, would be at their backs.

It was hot. Dandy found a spot on the stern where the breeze blew over the deck and sprawled out. Spencer and Jake climbed into the cockpit with Scott, and they set off under a cloudless sky.

Jake, who was to take Cliff's place as topside man during the dive, was an agreeable companion. He'd crewed in the races off Nantucket Sound and didn't need to be told what to do. They set the jib, and Jake winched in the sheets to get the most from the breeze, which came in quivering fits and starts.

Down-channel, Scott observed, the ripples petered out completely. "Our wind isn't going to hold."

Jake nodded. He was clearly enjoying himself. "I'll bet she flies in a good one."

Scott held much pride in the *Picaroon*, since he'd built her himself, and the big man's praise boosted his spirits, which had been running pretty low after the business with Billy.

Jake talked quietly about his own experiences, about demasted sloops and the squalls that hit without warning in the more open waters of the Atlantic. He was a well-informed man, and Scott enjoyed his company. Jake had learned how to sail in the little flatties on the Charles River when he'd studied law at Harvard.

"A lawyer in police work?"

He'd given up a law practice for personal reasons, he said, and from the distant look that came over his face, Scott had the idea an unhappy memory lurked in the past, one that didn't invite prying.

Spencer hadn't said much of anything since they'd started. Hands in his pockets, he stood in the well and seemed to lose himself in the trough of a wave. As they came out of Griffin Bay, he suddenly lightened up. "Mind if I take the wheel?"

"It's yours," Scott said.

Spencer ran a wandering course down San Juan Channel, deliberately oversteering at times, trying to make the most of the wind. Dacron rustled and snapped as the sails luffed and filled in the faltering wind.

"No danger of being overpowered," Jake said.

Spencer nodded. "Too bad we don't have forty-knot winds. I'd like to put her gunwales under."

"Living on the edge, is it?" Jake said.

Spencer smiled and leaned on the wheel. "That's what it's all about."

Off Turn Rock the wind picked up as it so often did coming out of Upright Channel, and a small burst filled the sails. Water broke over the bow and sprayed the cockpit with fountains of stinging foam. Jake gave thumbs-up approval and, laughing, said, "Maybe you're going to get your wish, Senator."

The wind direction shifted, and Spencer ran her into Upright Channel. They gathered speed to six knots.

"Ready about," Spencer shouted, and turned her nose into the wind. "Hard a lee!"

Jake let go the jib sheet, and the jib sail fluttered as the *Picaroon* ran head to wind. The sail flopped as the boom swung over. Scott winched her in, and they ran close-hauled on a new tack. Wind and spray splashed Scott's face, blotting out trouble, stirring up dreams, and for the first time in days, Scott felt the warm glow of contentment.

At Wasp Passage they ran out of wind. Becalmed, they handed down the sails, and Scott started up the engine.

"Where we headed?" Spencer said, showing his first real interest in their destination.

"I thought we'd try Jones Island. There's a good dive there. I tried it once few months back. Seems uncomplicated. Might even get some scallops for dinner."

Spencer nodded agreement with the plan, and they set a course for Jones.

They dropped anchor in a small cove just south of Spring Pass and lowered the rubber raft over the side. Spencer dug his equipment out of his bag and began laying it out on the bunk, carefully separating the pieces he'd brought for Cliff from his own. Scott looked at the assortment of gear and a warning bell went off in his head. All brand new. Labels still on them.

How long had it been since Spencer had made a dive? Maybe years. A diver who went only at long intervals quickly came under the novice category. Scott studied him with a frown. So little flesh on his bones, eyes deeply shadowed, cheeks that blended too well with his ash-colored hair. Clearly he wasn't in the peak of condition, and this could make even a simple dive hazardous.

"Everything's here," Spencer said, grinning proudly at the equipment laid out in front of him.

It was. Neoprene wet suit with nylon lining, the quarter-inch thickness necessary for these waters where the temperature generally ranged between a cold thirty-eight to forty-two degrees. The buoyancy compensator backpack and the diver's life-support line — the regulator with the combo gauge to read air pressure, water temperature, and depth; weights; booties; gloves; fins; and snorkel for surface swimming.

About all that was missing was a speargun. For this, at least, Scott was much relieved. Suddenly he felt like a diving instructor facing a reckless fledgling, and he wondered, Should he call the whole thing off?

"What do you think?" Spencer said.

Jake whistled. "Bet it didn't come cheap."

"Mmm," Scott said, trying to hide his concern. "Looks good. Let's check it out." Scott ran his finger along the hose. No nicks he could see. The mouthpiece was clear. He pressed the inflator on the buoyancy vest. It worked. He'd already run a check on Spencer's air tank. According to the boys at the Underwater Shop in Friday Harbor, it was full at a reading of three thousand pounds per square inch, sufficient under normal conditions for an hour's dive. "How much weight are you wearing?"

"Eighteen pounds."

Scott studied Spencer's scrawny frame. Fifteen pounds ought to do it.

Equipment-wise, Spencer was ready. Physically, even mentally, Scott held grave doubts. "I think it might be wise to take it real easy this first time out," he cautioned.

Jake nodded firm approval.

But Spencer wasn't in a cautious frame of mind. "Hey, Scottie, don't go chicken on me."

"Look," Scott said, annoyed, "I've been in surgery for better than two months. Haven't made a dive in over three. How long has it been for you?"

Spencer shrugged and didn't answer.

Jake went to work securing the raft to the stern cleats and dropping buoy flags to warn boaters that divers were under the surface. He seemed to know just what to do, Scott thought gratefully.

Scott outlined the dive plan while Spencer suited up. "Thirty minutes for the first run. There's a rock ledge at about thirty feet. Bottom comes up at the base of a long slope. Bottom is mud and sand to the east, rocky with lots of barnacles and seaweed to the west."

"How deep?"

"Goes to a max of about ninety feet."

Spencer nodded enthusiastically.

"If we try the bottom, we'll have to keep it short," Scott warned. "Ten minutes. Gets us away from decomp time." He knew Spencer understood about the nitrogen buildup in deep water that caused the bends.

Scott wiggled into his Farmer John suit and answered Jake's questions about emergency procedures. "If you hear a bang against the keel, it'll be us. If problems develop topside, you bang and we'll come. Whatever you do, don't let the boat drift."

"I could try to follow you in the raft," Jake said. Dandy watched, tail wagging slowly.

Scott pondered. The cove had twists and bends and a long rock reef that jutted out from Jones Island, serving as a breakwater for the bay. If they fell off course, it would be handy to have a boat nearby. It would mean less surface swimming, which, for a diver, could be exhausting and potentially dangerous. But following a dive from the surface wasn't all that easy. "Might be more trouble than it's worth," Scott said. "We'll stay with the anchor line. We should be okay." He looked to see if Spencer was listening, but he was standing near the side rail, struggling with his backpack.

"Could someone help with this buckle?"

Jake climbed over the cabin hatch and helped him strap the air tank to his back.

"It's slack tide," Scott said. "Gives us most of an hour before the current picks up. We want to watch it, though. Sometimes you can get a rip in here." A strong current could carry them a long distance from their entry point. "There's some thick bull kelp to the south. You'll want to get under it. Whatever you do, don't fight it."

Spencer's grin said he thought all the warnings unnecessary. He fit his mask over his face and tested the mouthpiece, gave the thumbs-up sign, and stood poised to go. Head and body cloaked in a thick black skin with tubes coming out of his mouth and squirreling over his head, the snorkel standing up like a deer's antler past his temples, tank hanging to his buttocks, he looked like a small spaceman with fins.

"Now remember, we're on the buddy system, and that means you never lose sight of me and I never lose sight of you."

Spencer nodded impatiently.

Scott studied the direction of the sun's rays as they penetrated the water almost directly overhead. The current—only very slight now—ran gently from east to west. "Thirty minutes," he reminded Spencer. "Go down the anchor line. Dive into the current."

But Spencer, holding onto the mask with one hand and his mouthpiece with the other, was already flipping backward off the side of the boat. Scott could only follow.

11

It was always a shock, that initial impact with the water, like sliding through ice. It took your breath, froze the muscles. Scott worked to relax, not allow the cold water filling up the inside of his suit to cause him to tense up. He took slow, even breaths, waited for the numbing pain to go away, for the temperature of his body to warm the water and insulate him from the cold.

He rolled and stretched, kicked lightly until the muscles in his body went limp, and, warmed again, he imagined himself a gull soaring on a pocket of wind. Bubbles filled the water above him, streaming upward in a blue and yellow cloud to catch the sunlight. Scott tracked their rise, which he calculated would be just under the anchor line of the *Picaroon*. Off to the north, the kelp waved gently. He swam toward it.

The water was clear, with direct sun overhead and no clouds. He guessed his range of visibility to be fifty feet, although he knew perceptions under the water could be deceiving, sometimes causing divers to estimate distances inaccurately and dive deeper than was safe. Ahead, he saw Spencer finning his way toward a large rock ledge, maybe twenty feet distant. He twisted and dove and disappeared in a forest of kelp. Scott started after him.

A school of minnows darted by. Scott kicked his heels and

descended under the blanket of kelp. Colors turned from red and orange to muted blues and greens. The speckled top of a blue cod swam under him. Scott slipped through the wispy lower layers of kelp. Tiny beads of plankton floated around him like dust particles trapped in the thin shaft of sunlight that eluded the brown tangles of seaweed.

The depth gauge on his regulator said he was at thirty-five feet. The rock shelf lay just ahead. He couldn't see Spencer. Green and purple sea urchins nestled in the rocks, their stubby spines sticking out like porcupines. Still no Spencer.

He explored the rock crevices that sloped downward, annoyed that Spencer wasn't following the buddy system of keeping each other in sight. Then he spotted him, twisting and flying like a leaf just turned free in the wind, reaching out, touching and testing, as a child might gather up chocolate creams in a candy store. Spencer had always loved to dive, and Scott knew the exhilaration he was feeling this moment, floating in a world without wind, listening to the soft, echoing sounds of his own breathing.

Spencer started down the rock slope. Scott swam along the edges, tracking his descent. A Tiger Rockfish erected its spiny fins in front of him and, like a sea bandit, flitted back into a crevice. All around him were the veiled outline of the underwater cliffs. Scott thought of something Al had said about the dig. "Glaciers gouging deep valleys and mountains falling into the sea." So it was. Boulder and rock formations were thickly populated with sea urchins and lush plant life. He was seeing the geological beginnings of the islands.

He swam down to another ledge, scanned the slope to the bottom. Spencer was still exploring on his own, having a good time. Scott checked his depth. Fifty feet. Another forty to the bottom. He checked the watch on his left wrist. They'd been down twenty minutes. He wondered if Spencer remembered. Ten more minutes.

He added a small amount of air to his buoyancy vest, flicked his ankles, and went off the ledge, almost like a skydiver soaring through space. He finned a steep trail down, reached out along the way to touch the thorny husks of mussels growing in the jagged face of the rocks.

Halfway, willowy white arms floated out of the rocks and interrupted his descent. A large octopus stared back at him through the small black eyes that were lodged in the umbrella lump that was the center of its amorphous body. It must have measured thirty feet from tip to tip. Its long tentacles floated gracefully around it like the arms of a ballerina, never quite coming to rest. Scott backed away to give it more room. Unless bothered, this was a shy creature that would withdraw from a confrontation altogether.

The creature wafted about, turned from milky white to russet, a sign it had been frightened by the encounter, and stole quietly back into the rocks. Scott swam on. In seconds his fin touched mud and sent up a yellow cloud. When the silt settled, he saw Spencer. He was only a few feet away, but he was no longer swimming freely, exploring the community of creatures that flourished on the bottom of this tidal pool. He was holding onto his mask, face turned up, kicking fiercely, and Scott knew immediately that he was in trouble.

His eyes through his mask were widely dilated. He made the chop sign under his throat, which meant he was out of air. But Scott had checked the tanks before the dive. They'd been full at three thousand pounds per square inch. It was inconceivable he could be out of air so soon.

Scott signaled to see if the mouthpiece was fouled. Spencer's head moved back and forth frantically, indicating that wasn't the problem. He was out of air. Worst of all, he looked desperate.

Scott pointed to his own mouthpiece. They would go up sharing his air. Spencer seemed to understand, which meant at least he was still functioning. Much relieved, Scott held his mouthpiece firmly so as to keep control and placed it into Spencer's hand. He waited for him to take two breaths. Thousands of bubbles erupted over them. Spencer was breathing too rapidly, showing signs of panic. If he didn't slow down, he'd lose too much carbon dioxide

71

and hyperventilate. If he didn't slow down, at this depth and in this ice-cold water, he'd markedly increase the air consumption. If Scott couldn't get him to relax, he would use up all their air, and they'd both drown in the rocky depths of the cove. Scott felt a sudden chill.

He put his free hand on Spencer's wrist and pressed it firmly, tried to reassure him, to tell him all would be well if they kept their heads. Spencer gulped in air and paid no attention. Scott gave the signal that everything was all right and waited while Spencer took another breath. Waited. Then exhaled slowly while Spencer continued to suck in air. The cold began to penetrate Scott's arms and legs, and he knew it was time to move.

He recovered the mouthpiece, cleared it, and inhaled, trying not to breathe too fast. Spencer watched anxiously. Scott took another breath, resisting the strong temptation to gulp it in. He returned the mouthpiece to Spencer, who took it eagerly, and they started up. Scott kept a firm grip on the regulator.

Kicking heels, they rose, like two men climbing a rope, face to face, knees sometimes getting in the way, bubbles gurgling all around like the jet in a hot tub. Both breathing off one tank, it was slow and cumbersome, and although every instinct told them to shoot straight to the surface, to prevent nitrogen buildup they could go no faster than the smallest bubbles rising above them.

They rose to the first ledge and paused. Spencer was breathing almost normally. *Good. He's relaxing.* They ascended another twenty feet. Scott looked at the compass on his right wrist and saw a new problem. They were off course from their entry point. The tide must have carried them. He determined they needed to go in a northwesterly direction. It meant more time underwater, but was safer when one considered the option, swimming on top of the water encumbered by gear, a long distance from their boat, both exhausted. He motioned they must change direction. Spencer shook his head and pointed straight up. Either he'd lost his sense of direction — easy to do underwater — or he was on the edge of panic again.

Scott's watch showed they'd been down nearly forty minutes. His pressure gauge indicated his tank registered near the empty mark. Spencer's first breaths on Scott's tank had been excited. He'd used up more of the air by breathing too fast. They still had enough to get to the surface, but none to spare, none to spend arguing over the direction they should take.

Scott took the mouthpiece, breathed in, and started up, following his compass, looking for the anchor line that had been set in the sand and rocks near shore at about a thirty-foot depth. Spencer had no choice. He had to go along.

They traveled a short distance until they ran into long strings of kelp growing up from the last ledge. No anchor chain, but the sun sent a dim trail of light from the surface that meant they were moving on course. Now the problem was staying under the kelp, not coming up until they were well out of it, for the kelp tended to thicken near the surface, throwing a blanket of twine over the top of the water, and Scott wasn't ready to risk more problems.

He swam in the direction he thought would keep them clear of it, the direction he felt sure would lead them to the anchor chain. It was due north and then west. Spencer pulled back and pointed straight up. Clearly, he saw the extra distance as an impediment to getting out of the water, and all he wanted was to get out, the shortest way possible. Scott shook his head and pointed west. Spencer ripped the mouthpiece from Scott's hand and started up, pulling Scott after him.

They floated through the first of it, the long spindly stalks like the base of trees. Spencer still held the mouthpiece as they continued up into denser strands that began to resemble limbs and branches, on up into thickets, like vines.

As Scott had feared, the finger-sized strands hooked their tanks, snarled around their hoses, snared their legs and arms. It was time to drop his weight belt, get more buoyancy, but he couldn't get his arms free to release it. Couldn't reach his knife, either, although cutting their way out was a last resort. Much quicker to slip out.

Beside him, Spencer, bound up in kelp, squirmed and thrashed, using up the precious air and getting himself more firmly entangled in the hundreds of strands that fanned across the surface. Above them, through the forest of dark weeds, the sun sent a veiled trail of light. They were close—very close. If they could hold on just a little longer.

Scott wiggled until he was able to slip his hand down to his calf and remove the knife sheathed there. He cut away at the slippery twines. Beside him, Spencer flailed and pulled at his mask. The mouthpiece spit free. Scott slipped it into his own mouth, breathed in. Nothing. Now he knew the beginnings of real terror.

He told himself he must slow down, keep his head. He exhaled, knew he had to subsist on the air remaining in his lungs, tried to move, but he and Spencer were tied together in the interlacing strings of kelp. Above them only a foot or two—sunlight and air. If he could just work his way out slowly . . . The trouble was Spencer was fighting it, entangling them all the more.

Scott exhaled and cut through the rubbery layers of brown vegetation, telling himself he'd be all right if he didn't rush, if he didn't panic. He kicked lightly. Not too hard or he'd wrap it around tighter. Didn't take long. Seemed endless. The twines began to separate. Pieces of it floated away. He wanted to hold his breath. Knew he mustn't. Knew he had to breathe out, counting on the reserve air in his lungs.

Spencer made a frantic thrust, clutched Scott around the neck and boosted himself up, toward the sun, pushing Scott down, tangling them up again in the seaweed. He felt a stabbling pain in his chest. He couldn't hold on any longer. He reached for the release on Spencer's weight belt, unlocked it. The weights sank. His lungs bursting, he dropped his own weights and felt them both lift.

All at once Spencer stopped struggling. He didn't move at all. Scott kicked gently, fins stuck in the twine. The pain in his chest traveled to his abdomen and back to his throat. Couldn't exhale anymore. Lungs wanted to burst. He wiggled. One last time. The kelp released them. Scott shot out of the water, pulling Spencer with him.

He gulped in fresh air, swallowed water strongly laced with salt, choked on it, coughed, tried to get another breath, choked again, spit out water, took another breath, and gagged. Spencer slipped from his grasp, started down. Scott caught hold of his tank, pulled him back. But Spencer still wasn't moving.

All around them, water, choppy and foaming. In the distance the sharp edge of the reef rising off to the southwest. They'd gone much farther than Scott had thought and surfaced a long distance from their entry point. They were out in open waters, far from Jake and the *Picaroon,* and from the looks of the sea, wind and tide were putting out some good-sized waves. He'd brought them up from the bottom, but with Spencer unconscious beside him, and in unprotected waters, they were a long way from being out of trouble.

12

Spencer wasn't breathing. The air hadn't stimulated his brainstem to start his respiration again, not a good sign. He floated faceup, showing no signs of life. If his heart had stopped they were in big trouble for here on the water, rolling in the chop, a cardiac massage was out of the question.

Scott looked around in desperation. The fir-covered cliffs of Orcas Island rose to the east, a thousand yards or better. No one in sight. The reef ran along to his west, shutting off the bay where the *Picaroon* lay at anchor. Slime-covered rocks cropped up out of the falling tide, a good two hundred yards distant. No boaters. Far off across the wide body of water to the north, a pair of cruisers headed toward the yellowed outline of Speiden Island. Too far for them to see his frantic arm signals. He yelled. Took in water. Yelled again. Nothing but the swash and gurgle of the water. Spencer needed help, and Scott was all there was.

Scott released the shoulder and waist strap on his scuba and jettisoned his tank. The gauge on Spencer's tank still read half full. Had Spencer been wrong? A fouled mouthpiece, perhaps, and he'd panicked. Then he thought, What if Spencer doesn't make it? Leroy and the coroner would need to know. He decided not to drop Spencer's tank.

He partially inflated Spencer's vest and his own. With the weights and his tank jettisoned and the buoyancy of the vests, he could now work on Spencer without fear of sinking. He peeled off the rubber gloves and pressed a bare finger on Spencer's neck. The carotid pulse was faint but definitely there. The heart hadn't quit yet.

Encouraged, he began the arduous task of giving mouth-to-mouth resuscitation. Tossing about in the sea, buoyed up by his vest, he cupped a hand around Spencer's mouth, pinched his nose shut, covered his mouth with his own, and breathed in, paused, breathed in again. He timed them, twelve to a minute.

Spencer's chest rose and fell as the air filled his lung cavity and expelled itself. Slow and even. Scott tried not to think about the cold or that he was tired and struggling to get his own breath. A wave bounced them up, moved them farther out into open waters. Water splashed over his hood and dripped off his nose onto Spencer's cheeks. Spencer didn't move.

He blew air into Spencer's lungs, looked around for help. No one. Across Spring Pass a wall of twisted firs and madronas grew out of the rocks. Beside him a gull landed on a floating piece of driftwood. Whitecaps on the waves. No boats.

Time dragged as they bounced around in the chop. Scott blew air into Spencer's mouth and counted. Three minutes. Four. A chill crept over him. He shivered, couldn't feel his toes. The bright silver body of a salmon hurtled into the air, struck the water like a skipping rock, splashed up foam. Still no boats.

Five minutes and Spencer wasn't breathing on his own. If he didn't begin soon, it would all be pointless. What was it—eight minutes? Ten? If he didn't breathe on his own by then there was practically no chance of pumping enough blood to stimulate the brain cells. Brain dead. Restore the breathing for an everlasting world of gray.

The eddies swirled the water into spinning whirlpools. The current was building. Seven minutes. Scott couldn't stop. Textbook cases were no help here. He had to go on with it no matter how long it took. He kept breathing into Spencer's mouth. More cruisers. Long way off. He blew air. The pain in his chest worsened.

Water flew up, thick with salt and foam, and cascaded over them. Bitterly cold. He sealed the cup around Spencer' mouth and continued to breathe. Going on eight minutes. Was it already too late?

It started as a cough, like an engine not getting enough gas. Spencer sputtered. Scott continued blowing in air. The sputtering turned into choking and coughing. The engine fired, fitfully, then quickly, his chest rising and falling. Spencer began breathing on his own. He didn't open his eyes. He'd been without air too long and had lost body heat, but he was breathing. He was alive.

"Take it easy, Spence. We made it this far. Just have to get back to the boat." It was unlikely Spencer heard, but saying the words helped Scott. They'd jumped two hurdles. Only one to go.

Afternoon tide changes often stirred up the breezes in the islands. They'd started their dive in calm seas. Now, here, outside the reef, the waves were building. Farther out in the channel, they ran big, crested with glistening white peaks. They still had some distance to cover to reach the *Picaroon*, and Spencer was still unaware, still unable to propel himself. Scott's legs and arms were numb from the cold, and the pain in his chest told him they'd both been in the water too long.

His best bet, he decided, was to go for the reef, find a high spot where they could sit it out until Jake or a passing boater found them. There was one problem with this plan. The waves had carried them farther out to sea, and by his calculations they were still at least three hundred yards from the reef. Swimming, pulling

Spencer along, he couldn't snorkel his way, using his natural buoyancy. He would have to swim with Spencer, dragging against the forces of the wind and seas. He wasn't at all sure he was up to it.

A wave rolled toward them. "Hang on," Scott said to an unresponding Spencer.

The wave picked them up, carried them forward, rolled them back down. Scott got the worst of it. He tasted salt, spit it out. He fit his mask back over his face and blew into the mouthpiece as a mountain of water spilled over their heads.

Spencer drifted a few feet. Scott followed, caught hold of the air valves, and, pulling the tank with Spencer on his back, started out. The waves drove them back. Stroke after stroke, he fought the whirling seas. The pain in his chest intensified. He took a deep breath, another, swallowed more water. Tried to spit it out, waited for the nausea to go away, took in more water. His lungs filled up with it. His fingers clutched Spencer's tank so tightly the steel edges on the reserve valve dug into his flesh. He ought to have felt pain. He felt nothing.

Spencer's head drooped. His lips were blue. Another roller struck, and more salt water sloshed into Scott's mouth, slid down his throat. He swallowed, gagged, spit, struggled to hold onto the tank, and sank deeper into the water. The air in his lungs was running out. He had to keep moving.

Across the immediate horizon the jagged edges of the rocks broke through the surf. Not far, he thought. Two hundred yards to the reef and on the other side, the indented shoreline of Jones Island and the cove. It might as well have been a hundred miles. Here, with the water slapping them about and Spencer still unconscious, he could go no farther.

Another plunging wave rolled toward them, peaked and showered them with salt foam. They were in plain sight of the rocks and dozens of boats heading north into Speiden Channel, in trouble, and no one knew.

Scott was thirty-seven and reasonably fit. Spencer was three or four years older and not in very good condition at all. At this point, however, both their chances were equally grim. Without their wet suits, in these cold waters, they'd have been goners long before this. Their weight belts jettisoned and with the natural buoyancy of the suit and vest, it was unlikely they'd sink—not right away at least. But the cold was beginning to permeate the layers of nylon and neoprene. Scott felt the chills going from his toes to his chest. It was taking more breaths just to take a stroke. It looked as though they would perish from the loss of body heat before they ever drowned.

To slip to the bottom of the sea where a diver out for adventure, like himself, might come upon you might be a fitting way to die if you had to die, but to float to your death on the top of the waves and be hauled out like a dead fish, like Red Thompson, filled him with an unreasoning horror.

Scott shifted his grip on Spencer's tank and bit down determinedly. "We're headed for the reef."

He struck out again. It seemed hours thrashing about in the waves, a lifetime since they'd dived off the side of the *Picaroon* to explore the waters at the bottom of the cove, yet by Scott's watch it had been just under sixty minutes, less than twenty minutes since they'd surfaced and he'd blown breath back into Spencer's lungs, a few moments since he'd begun the struggle to get back to land.

His thoughts wandered. Was it hot in North Carolina? It was cold here. Wouldn't be cold with Erin pressed against his chest. An image of her appeared on the tossing foam. Her soft hair brushed against his chin. "You see," she said, as they floated around the dance floor, "you're a wonderful dancer. . . ."

"And you," he said, grinning back at her, "are quite crazy."

She laughed that light little laugh and cuddled closer.

A wave slapped him in the face, and he felt Spencer start to slide from his arms. He hauled him back in, swam on. He couldn't feel his hands or his feet. Wanted to go on dancing with Erin. Too tired. He swam into the chop, getting sleepy. The land grew fuzzy. No closer. The rocks were no nearer. Water piling up.

An object flickered under the strong rays of the sun. Something bounced toward them, moving on the crest of the waves. He raised the mask, eyes flickered awake. He strained to see. Looked awfully like a boat. He tried to shout, took in more water. Nothing came out. Had they seen? They moved closer. He tried to lift his arm to signal, sank under a roller, Spencer with him. He fought back up. The boat continued toward them. Two forms rose from her deck.

Scott pulled on the tank, made one last try to get the boaters' attention. The pain in his chest was much worse. His legs knotted painfully. Couldn't move at all. Whoever was in that boat had better get here quickly.

He was still holding onto Spencer's tank, head out of the water, mask off, when the boat slid in beside them. It wasn't a cruiser. It was much smaller. He looked up, not fully focusing. Saw the shapes of a dog and a man, heard the excited bark, felt strong hands grabbing him, powerful arms lifting him. He looked up into the dark concerned face. It was Jake with Dandy in the rubber raft.

"Just take it easy," Jake said. "I'm going to pull you both back to the boat. Don't you worry," the gentle Georgian voice said soothingly, "you're going to be all right."

13

Jake ran lines off the stern of the raft and dragged Scott and Spencer like a couple of whales. It took them only five minutes to reach the *Picaroon*. They'd been less than three hundred yards away, but completely hidden by the reef and the swells on the sea.

Scott tried to help Jake. His arms felt like lead weights, couldn't raise them over his head. He more or less floated against the rubber sides of the raft while Jake unloaded Spencer's tank and hoisted

Spencer onto the deck of the *Picaroon.* Then Jake pulled Scott up, and, kneeling in the well, they both went to work on Spencer, got his wet suit off, and began rubbing his arms and legs.

"G-got to g-get him warm," Scott stuttered.

Spencer moved, sputtered like a man waking from a drunken stupor, and began to shake. Jake broke out the blankets from the bunk and wrapped them around him.

"Ma-maybe s-some brandy," Scott suggested.

"Where do you keep it?"

"F-foot l-locker. U-under the bunk."

Jake found the brandy, and they tried to pour some into Spencer's mouth. It dripped down his chin. A few drops seeped in, and Spencer stirred again.

"M-more," Scott said.

Spencer choked, opened his eyes, and looked up at them fuzzily. "Scottie?"

"Just take it easy," Jake said.

Scott left Spencer to Jake's capable ministerings and went below to change. He struggled out of his wet suit and pulled on his pants. Dandy watched. "I—I'm okay, boy," he reassured the dog. Dandy licked his face and settled at his feet. Still chilled, Scott pulled a wool sweater over his shirt and returned to the deck. He couldn't stop shaking.

Jake poured another glass of brandy. "I think you need some of this."

Scott drank. It burned all the way down, settled warmly in his stomach. "Much better, thanks."

Jake stared at Scott's hands. "You're bleeding."

Scott was surprised to see the deep cuts on the undersides of his fingers where he'd gripped Spencer's tank. Curiously, he felt no pain.

"Shall I bandage them?"

"The air should take care of it."

Jake grinned. "You're the doctor."

"And now you mention it, I think we better get Spence to a hospital."

Spencer had been leaning against the cabin bulkhead, watching quietly, but on the word "hospital" sat up, excited. "No!"

"You were unconscious out there," Scott said. "You're doing fine now, but we should check your cardiac and kidney functions, make certain you don't have any future problems."

Spencer shook his head in firm rejection. He knew hospitals, and they'd keep him for days, he said. This would foul up the schedule.

Scott guessed it had more to do with appearances than schedules. A senator in the hospital would bring a lot of unwanted conjecturing by the media. Scott argued, but finally, convinced nothing would change Spencer's mind, he gave up.

For the next half hour they lay out quietly on the deck of the *Picaroon,* rocking at anchor while they let the sun perform its healing miracles. Jake talked about the boats that had paraded through Pole Pass, going around the south end of Jones Island.

"And we missed them all," Scott said. "How did you find us?"

"When you didn't come up for so long, I knew something was wrong, but it was really Dandy, here, who put me onto looking on the other side of the rocks." Jake roughed up Dandy's fur. "He wanted to jump off the raft and swim over there, and finally I got smart and went the way he wanted, saw you floundering around."

"So glad you did," Scott said with feeling.

Until now Jake had concerned himself only with getting them warm. Now it was his turn to ask questions. "What happened down there?"

Scott explained about the air in Spencer's tank.

Spencer listened, confused. He had no recollection of anything after the first part of the dive.

"The part that's hard to understand," Scott said, "is that I had that tank checked out myself. It was full. It would be just about impossible to use it all up in such a short time."

Jake stepped over the well and walked along the rail to the stern where they'd left Spencer's tank. Jake examined it, returned after a few minutes. "Still registers better than half full."

Scott nodded. "I know."

"Could be a faulty valve."

"Where did you get your equipment?" Scott asked Spencer.

"Skin Divers in Seattle. Bought it just before we drove up."

The tank had been properly packed by the shop, and so it was equally hard to imagine damaging it in the short drive to the ferry landing. Scott shook his head. "Factory problem more than likely."

Jake didn't say anything, but it set Spencer off about there not being enough teeth in the present consumer protection law and he'd do something about that in the next session of the Congress. Scott didn't see how more legislation would have prevented the problem with the tank, but Spencer seemed to enjoy finding someone to blame.

After a time he got off the subject of corporate responsibility and, leaning back against the cabin bulkhead, face turned up to catch the sun, began to remember what had happened on the dive.

"I found a scallop bed. I was just coming to get you, Scottie. Then I started breathing in water. Nearly choked to death. Scared the shit out of me."

"Water?" Jake said, puzzled.

Spencer nodded. "Guess I went a little crazy. I wanted to tear off the mask, get out. I thought the whole ocean was closing in on me."

Jake grew silent, and Scott guessed he was thinking about Spencer sucking in water. A flaw in the mouthpiece or the hose? There was another possibility. Maybe someone had tampered with the tank? But who? Made no sense.

When Spencer went below to get a sweater, Scott told Jake he planned to take the tank in to the shop in the morning to check it out again. Jake nodded approval. The air leak, if that's what it was, might have been an accident, but Scott knew what the big security man was thinking. They couldn't rule out the possibility it might have been a deliberate attempt on Spencer's life.

*   *   *

Cliff and Gwen had spent the afternoon golfing. Back from the course, the two of them were in the living room, drinking tea and laughing about their game when Scott, Spencer, and Jake dragged in, looking, Scott feared, as though they'd been to the wars. Spencer, particularly. His face was sallow, his eyes more sunken than usual.

Gwen took one look and drew in her breath. "What happened?"

"Nothing," Spencer said in a grumpy voice.

"Got to be something. You look terrible."

"We had a little problem with one of the tanks. No big deal."

Gwen walked over to him and touched his arm. "I knew you shouldn't dive. It's been too long. I—I had a feeling."

Spencer shook off her hand. "Don't be stupid. And for God's sake, Gwen, stop hovering." He dropped into Scott's big leather chair.

Gwen sat down on the fireplace hearth, looking thoroughly rebuffed.

Cliff bit down. Annoyed with Spencer, Scott explained to Gwen what had happened to her husband, leaving out that he'd been unconscious.

"You see," Spencer said, with the edge still in his voice. "I was never in any real danger."

Jake had been looking out the window, trying, Scott guessed, to stay clear of Spencer's family affairs. But when he turned and looked down at Gwen, there was sympathy in the gentle face. "And how was the golf this afternoon?" he asked.

She perked up. "I shot an eighty-five. Can you believe?"

Jake grinned. "I believe."

"A birdie on the fifth hole," Cliff joined in enthusiastically. He and Jake joked about Gwen's golf, and Spencer sat broodingly, buried in the big chair, saying nothing.

Everyone was laughing when Spencer broke in. "Cliff, do you think we have a news item here?"

Cliff's eyes behind the heavy framed glasses were surprised. "On the golf?"

Spencer sighed impatiently. "The dive."

Cliff's glasses fell forward on his nose. "You want to run a story that you nearly drowned?" He shoved the glasses back.

"Wasn't exactly what I had in mind."

"I hope you weren't thinking of saying *you* rescued Scott," Gwen said.

Spencer's face flamed. "Of course not."

Gwen picked up her teacup and walked into the kitchen.

"Print whatever you like," Scott said, "but leave my name out of it."

"Scottie," Spencer said in a wounded voice, "politics is a large part public image. I hope you don't think I enjoy it."

"*Your* image, Spence. I'm a surgeon, remember, and publicity is bad for *mine*."

"Forget it," Spencer said to Cliff, and walked out on the deck to stare sulkily off at the water.

Looking uncomfortable, Jake and Cliff decided to go for a walk on the beach.

"I'm sorry," Gwen said after they left. "Spencer forgets sometimes, but I know he's grateful." She touched Scott's hand again. "We both are."

At dinner, Spencer and Gwen appeared to have patched it up. Spencer was his talkative self again as they sat around the big game table in the living room, he and Gwen cozying up to each other. In his vibrant tenor voice, Spencer described to Gwen and the rest of them the white and yellow anemones he'd seen on the dive.

"Snow-white flowerlike clusters hanging off the rocks. You can't imagine until you've been there."

"Sounds beautiful," Gwen said.

Cliff poked at his salad with his fork. "I understand, like jelly fish—they sting."

Spencer didn't catch the sarcasm in Cliff's voice.

"That's pretty much mythical for Northwest anemones," he said and continued his descriptions, showing a surprising knowledge of the sea creatures and an astounding lack of perceptibility about Cliff. "Of course, even the anemone will move from danger, like any form of life."

"Been boning up, Spencer?" Scott said, amused.

Spencer laughed good naturedly. "A little. Didn't do me much good today, though, did it?" It was the first time he'd come close to admitting he'd been unprepared for the dive, and Gwen rewarded him with an affectionate smile. "Say, Scottie," Spencer said, "how about going fishing tomorrow?"

"You think you're up to it?"

"Absolutely."

Gwen's frown showed her instant concern. "Is it wise? After today?"

Spencer leaned over her chair and stroked her back. "Nothing dangerous about dropping a line over the side of a boat. I think you should go, too. Sea air will put some color in your cheeks." This was said humorously, since Gwen had a nice sunburn from the golf.

She smiled, and Cliff stabbed a piece of steak and didn't look up.

14

The grass dripped with morning dew when Scott loaded the air tank into the Jeep. He got only as far as the end of his drive, and Al flagged him down.

"You going to town?"

"Sure am. Want a lift?"

Al nodded. "Want to pick up a few items at the store."

The sun lit up the white peaks of Mount Baker as they rounded the curve by the lighthouse. Al had a sudden flash of memory.

"Almost forgot. I ran into Vic at the creek a few minutes ago. Said he wanted to talk to you."

"Is he still there?"

"No. He was going into town to talk to the sheriff. Said he'd see you there. Something about Billy, I believe."

"Anything hopeful?"

Al shrugged. "With that man, how can you tell?" Al looked on Vic as something of a wild person.

They drove the next half mile in silence. Across the strait the water stretched out, blue and still. The long shape of Vancouver Island toed out in the distance, and Victoria, the provincial capital of British Columbia, showed her sprawling silhouette against the morning sky. Scott remembered a day in the quaint old city last year when he and Erin had first come to know each other, and the memory stirred him.

"You hear anything from Erin, Al?"

"Talked to her last night, as a matter of fact. I have an idea she may be coming home soon."

Scott felt the familiar tug at his chest. "What makes you think that?"

But the old man just smiled one of those secret smiles and advanced no more information.

The prospect of Erin coming home had a remarkably buoyant effect on Scott's spirits. Across the yellowed slopes of Mount Finlayson, through the dried grass and stands of wind-twisted firs, he could almost smell the wild strawberries. It was going to be a good day, he thought happily, and somehow, they'd find a way to get Billy out of his troubles.

They left the mountain and started down the road by the dig. All the way to the blue waters of Griffin Bay the hillside was a mass of steeply carved mud squares. There were no students out yet. Too early.

Al stirred angrily. "Will you look at that. Unearthing all this beautiful land, and for what?"

"For history, Al," Scott said, grinning at the old man.

"Mmpf." Al scrunched down in his seat, annoyed into silence. He held that silence until they reached the airport road. A small Cessna swooped over them onto the airstrip, and Al turned chatty again. He expressed curiosity about the air tank. Scott knew he could trust the old man to keep a confidence, and he was interested in his opinion, so he told him about yesterday's troubles, leaving out how close they'd come to disaster.

Al picked up on it anyway. "Darned fool politician could've got you killed." Then he got off on one of his lectures about Scott taking too many chances and the foolhardiness of the young. Curiously, he didn't raise doubts about the cause of the tank failure, and Scott began to feel his own suspicions were unfounded.

Scott dropped Al at the store, left the air tank at the Underwater Shop, and went off to find Vic. He found him coming out of the sheriff's office, and he bubbled over with news.

Billy was free on bail. In fact, Billy had fished last night with the Indian boats, and word was he'd made a good catch. If it bothered Vic that he hadn't been given a day to make his own catch, he gave no sign of it, which showed the extent of his concern for Billy.

"Al said you heard something."

Vic nodded. "I'm getting to that. You remember Mike Armirez?"

"The purse seiner from Alaska who operates the *January*?"

"That's the one. Seems Mike was tied up next to Billy and Red the morning of the blockade. Mike's willing to swear he saw someone go aboard the *Judy Lynn* that morning."

"Can he describe this person?"

"Not exactly. He was looking through his port window. Only saw the legs. But he was absolutely certain whoever it was went on board Red's boat."

"Man or woman?"

"Man . . ." Vic paused. "Had to be a man."

"Big or small?"

"Medium, I think." Vic scratched his head, and Scott thought Vic's friend hadn't been sure.

88

"Did he notice anything unusual about him?"

"He was wearing jeans and those expensive deck shoes."

Nearly all the fishermen wore jeans, including Billy. Most of them wore boots or deck shoes and if they were new, they might look expensive to Vic's friend. "Did he see this man leave?"

"I asked him that, but I guess he got pretty busy about then. Course there was no reason for him to think it was important at the time. The point is, it's like Billy said. It proves Red saw someone on his boat that morning."

"Did you tell Leroy?"

"Yeah, but you know what a bonehead he can be."

What Vic wasn't saying was that Leroy had seen the obvious flaw in the story. Those legs could easily have belonged to Billy.

They were standing at the foot of Spring near where the masts and counting towers jammed up along the docks. Scott didn't want to deflate his friend. "Do you think Mike could remember more about the visitor if he put his mind to it?"

"I'll refresh his memory."

Scott left Vic and returned to the diving shop. The owner was waiting for him, and from his face, Scott knew he'd learned something that had upset him.

"I hope you know we can't assume responsibility in cases like this," he said.

"Cases like what? What was wrong with the tank?"

The diver pointed grimly to Spencer's aluminum air tank laid out on the table in front of him, shop tags hanging from its valves and a strip of blue plastic tape sticking to its undersurface. "There was nothing wrong with your tank or the regulator or the valves. The reason you ran out of air was someone filled it half up with water."

15

Scott drove home anxious to consult with Jake and found the house full of strangers. Cliff had apparently invited the media people for coffee, at Spencer's behest, and Madelyn and Dick Ellis, Robbie, Nancy, and their friends had invited themselves.

Scott walked in through the back door to avoid them and discovered Gwen in the kitchen nibbling on a piece of celery. A gentle breeze blew through the open window and out on the deck the lawn umbrellas Madelyn had imported for Spencer's coming reception wafted in the sun, unfamiliar faces under them.

"Always eat when I'm nervous," Gwen said. "Sorry about all this." She waved at the crowd in the living room and touched his arm softly. "If you don't want to go fishing today—if you have other plans—I hope you'll let Spencer know. We've taken terrible advantage of you, and it seems so wrong."

It was the first time since Spencer arrived that either of them had expressed genuine concern about Scott's plans. He was at once both forgiving and embarrassed. "No problem," he lied. Then he wondered, Should he tell Gwen about the tank? She seemed a sensible woman, who might persuade her husband to take more precautions. But would it be right to tell her before Spencer knew himself?

"Gwen! Come in here," Spencer called from the living room. "Someone here I want you to meet."

Gwen made a face. "I hate this," she whispered. Then, brushing her hand across Scott's arm, she put on her campaign smile and strolled into the living room. "I'm so pleased to know you," he heard her say in a cheerful voice, and he wondered if she actually hated it as much as she said.

Scott found Jake on the beach below the deck. Like two displaced persons, he and Dandy were wedged together companionably on a log just above the water's edge.

When Jake saw Scott he slipped back down to the sand. "What did you find out about the tank?"

"Someone filled it half up with water."

"Damn! I was afraid of something like that. Could it have been caused by a faulty valve?"

"No."

"You tell the senator?"

"He's tied up right now. Leroy wasn't in. I'll try him again."

"I could bring in more security people. Trouble is, I'm not sure it wouldn't make things worse. Something's different about this deal."

"Such as?"

"Who had access to the tank."

"I thought about that all the way home. Knowing how people on this island trust everyone, I imagine almost anyone could have tampered with it while it was in the shop."

"Did you tell the shop people the tank belonged to the senator?"

"No."

"Then don't worry about it."

Scott picked up a pebble and skipped it across the water. Jake threw one, too, and they watched it spit like a ricocheting bullet over the wavelets.

"What worries me is Spencer. I must have heard him mention our diving plans to over a dozen people the day he arrived, and I didn't know half of them."

91

Jake nodded. "And he seems to have made his share of enemies around here with the fishermen."

"Any ideas?"

"Let me think about it."

Scott returned to the house. Spencer was still in the living room talking to his guests. Scott called the sheriff. The dispatcher said he was on a case. Scott said he'd call back and rang off.

On the deck, Robbie and the girl from the dig huddled together on the bench rail in quiet conversation. It terminated abruptly when Scott walked over. A bee buzzed around the tray of doughnuts that sat on the table near Robbie. Scott reached for a doughnut and bit into it. "Nice day."

"Gorgeous," Robbie agreed. He introduced Scott to the girl.

Her name was Charleen Johnson. She was an island girl attending the state university and working at the dig for the summer. Her yellow hair fell straight over her shoulders, and she wore no makeup. Her face was burned red over brown from the sun. She wore white shorts and a brief top that showed off her deeply tanned shoulders and slender bronzed legs. She might have been beautiful, Scott thought, if she took any trouble about it.

"Do you like your work?" Scott asked.

"Very much." She had a nice even smile.

"To my inexperienced eyes, it looks like you're doing a great job."

"We try."

Robbie broke in with a comment that the senator's fall campaign plans were going well, which he said was typical. "The senator's a real pro." Charleen appeared content to let him do the talking, a role he clearly relished. His face flushed with enthusiasm as he talked about his work with the senator in the nation's capital. "It's a whole way of life. I've learned more from him in a few weeks than I learned in three years at State."

"Sounds as though you plan to run for office yourself someday."

He nodded vigorously. "Have to be at the national level, though. The real power's in Washington."

Scott wondered who the boy reminded him of.

"I'm planning law school next year. The senator says that's the way to go."

"Then will you join your father in the firm?"

Robbie laughed. "No way. I think he expects me to, but San Juan Island is a real dead end."

Charleen started down the stairs to the beach.

"Oops. Gotta go." Robbie winked knowingly. "Aren't many women on the island this summer. You have to make do."

Scott shook his head as he watched him run after the girl, thinking about that summer not so many years ago and realizing who Robbie reminded him of. He found it somehow depressing.

Scott wandered into the living room, hoping to catch Spencer, but found him surrounded by reporters still. He walked back to the bedroom to call Leroy again. The sheriff hadn't returned. Seeing the festivities would go on for some time, Scott decided to go down to the dock to install the downrigger on the runabout.

The runabout sat in the stall beside the *Picaroon,* tied firmly to the cleats with Al's familiar extra loop on the snapline. At Scott's insistence, Al had shared the small boat since Scott had acquired it the previous season. Scott smiled. The old boy had probably been out checking his crab pots again.

Scott surveyed the hull. The fiberglass was faded, and there were scuffs and signs of weathering on the cockpit housing. Needs a waxing, he thought. Another job to tackle when Spencer leaves.

It was boiling hot on the docks, and Scott stripped to his shorts while he worked with drill and screwdriver, fastening the big metal housing for the downrigger to the stern rail of the boat. A seagull landed on a piling nearby and watched while Scott cinched the plates into the wood and hooked up the wires.

After he'd drilled the new holes and made the connections, he lifted the lead ball to the transom. It weighed about thirty pounds, and it was work to get it into place, but that was the whole idea, to put sufficient weight on the line so it would sink straight down to the depth where they were most likely to find the fish. A short metal rod supported the weight. The fishing line would attach to the downrigger line, putting the fishing line deeper where the fish were, and the tripping device on the downrigger released it when a fish struck.

Unlike his old downrigger, this one was equipped with a footage counter that measured depth, and he was eager to try it. He dropped it over the side, checked the release clip on the line, and took a reading. Twelve feet. He smiled satisfaction. Better check the outboard. He connected the fuel line from the gas tank to the engine and hand-pumped fuel into the line. Then he put the key in the ignition and pushed the starter. After four sputtering tries, the motor turned over. He was pleased with his efforts.

Across the creek into Griffin Bay the water was flat. It was nearly slack tide. The fish would be running. If only Erin were here they could slip out and dangle their poles in congenial silence, just the two of them. Instead, there was Spencer.

Scott drew a deep sigh, looked at his watch. Nearly two o'clock. Surely Spencer would have finished with the media by now. He left the downrigger in the water and started back to the house.

Spencer was standing in the front doorway saying good-bye to Madelyn when Scott drove up. Hers was the only car left in the drive. Scott parked on the road and walked past her Honda unobserved into the breezeway by the carport. Madelyn and Spencer stood very close together. She was gazing into Spencer's eyes. He was telling her how wonderful she'd been about everything as only Spencer could. He leaned forward and kissed her cheek. Madelyn moved her face, and it turned into a brush of lips. Scott slipped in by the back door. Just inside, standing by the window looking out at Spencer and Madelyn, was a grim-faced Dick Ellis. Scott walked swiftly by. Behind him, the door clicked quietly open and shut.

Without all the people, the living room was strangely quiet.

"They all left," Gwen said cheerfully from her lounging position on the sofa. "Isn't it wonderful?"

The room was clear of everything. Even the coffee cups and

doughnut trays had disappeared, and the rug looked freshly vacuumed.

"Madelyn tidied up," Gwen said.

"Did a good job."

Gwen screwed up her nose. "Very efficient lady."

Scott wondered if Gwen guessed that Madelyn's interest in Spencer was more than that of one good Republican for another, but Gwen laughed, and Scott thought, Maybe she doesn't care.

"Where is everybody?"

"Cliff went to town on errands for Spencer. Jake's on the deck, and the others, I presume, have gone home."

Behind the sound of Madelyn's Honda rumbling out the drive, Spencer strode into the room, rubbing his hands together enthusiastically. "Ready?"

"Count me out," Gwen said, kicking off her shoes and tucking her feet under her. "I hate fishing."

"But you've never been," Spencer said.

"I know."

They smiled at each other, but there was the distance between them again that Scott had seen from the first, and Scott guessed another disagreement had caused Gwen to change her mind about the fishing. Life for Spencer and Gwen, it appeared, was a series of ups and downs.

16

It took another half hour to round up their gear, and Spencer dawdled trying to pick the proper lure. "Which do you think?" he said, holding up a plastic, flesh-colored plug and a bright silver flasher. "Take both and let's get going while the fish are still biting."

Dandy curled up in the cockpit beside Scott, and Jake and Spencer sat on the stern seat as they headed out of Fish Creek at trolling speed. The small boat slapped over the wavelets and splashed water in their faces. It was hot, and the cool salt spray felt good.

"Want to raise the downrigger?" Jake asked.

Impatient with delays, Scott said, "We'll run with it in the water. It's not far."

Spencer had been examining the boat critically from the start. Scott imagined on his Eastern Seaboard vacations, he was accustomed to going out in the big cruisers, and the runabout was a disappointment.

"Where did you get this little job, Scottie? Looks like it needs work."

"It was a barter deal."

Spencer laughed. "A seventeen-foot runabout for an appendix? Is that how medical costs are going these days?"

"More like a gall bladder and me coughing up eight grand to boot," Scott said, trying to hide his irritation, for jokes about surgeon's fees ran awfully thin on him these days.

Spencer looked truly surprised. "You were robbed. You could buy this on the market for half that."

Scott shrugged.

"That's what I love about this guy, Jake. He's a helluva sweet person, but a piss-poor businessman."

Scott shoved the stick forward, and a V-shaped wake kicked up white foam behind them as they built up speed.

"How do you like this, Jake?" Spencer shouted happily.

"I prefer sail, but it's pleasant."

Spencer held onto the side rail, leaned out, and caught the wind in his face. "Where's your sporting blood? A fast boat gets you where you want to go."

"What if you don't want to go anywhere?"

They ran at fifteen knots until they rounded Seal Rock, and Scott felt a slight pull on the rudder. He cut back on her speed.

"What's the matter?" Spencer said, frowning.

"A spun prop?" Jake guessed.

"No, I checked the prop last week. Feels like grass on her bottom. Probably needs a haul."

"Rev her up," Spencer suggested. "The force of the water should knock it off."

Scott ran her to eighteen hundred RPMs, and she squirrel-caged again. "Grass all right." He cut her speed to ten knots.

They reached the spot outside Scott's house where the little pleasure boats were starting to accumulate for the late afternoon fishing. Across the short fetch of water to Lopez, a quarry of terns and gulls carried on a squealing tussle over a run of candlefish. The sea was the brilliant azure blue of a bright summer day. Scott reduced to trolling speed, and they baited their hooks. They sat with their poles in the water, and in this relaxed atmosphere, Scott told Spencer what they'd discovered about the tank.

Spencer had panicked when he'd run out of air at the bottom of the bay, and so Scott had expected at least some handwringing when he told Spencer someone had deliberately fouled the tank. But Spencer barely reacted. He leaned back against the gunwale and said, "Water, huh?" as though he didn't fully comprehend. "So, someone really is trying to kill me."

Jake exchanged bewildered glances with Scott. "Don't worry, Senator, we're not going to let it happen."

Spencer's laugh was harsh. "How you going to stop it, Jake? They would have been successful this time if it hadn't been for Scottie."

Jake looked injured. "I'm sorry, Senator."

Scott lost all sympathy for his old classmate. "The only way to make sure it doesn't happen is to cancel your appearances here, and I believe both Jake and I suggested that."

Spencer went all smiles again and patted Jake on the back. "Hey, you're doing a great job. But hell, I can't run like a scared rabbit. I have obligations."

Maybe that was it. Spencer was half actor, after all. He was probably a good deal more upset than he let on.

They lost interest in fishing. They dangled their poles from the

97

holders while Scott ran the boat at trolling speed and steered in an aimless circle. Jake turned quiet, and Spencer spoke only when a new thought came to him.

"Who knows about the tank?"

"As far as I know, no one except the three of us and the owner of the Underwater Shop."

"How do you suppose it happened?"

"Quite simply, I imagine. Whoever did it filled it with water to make the air pressure check out full."

The lights suddenly went on in Spencer's head. He jerked up, mouth gaping open. "Wait a min-ute. You're saying this *couldn't* have happened at the factory, that someone *had* to have deliberately tampered with the tank?"

"That's *exactly* what I'm saying."

Now Spencer was shocked. "B-but who?" he murmured, as though the idea had only just sunk in. "Who would want to kill *me*?"

Spencer went into a quiet shell. Not easy to come to terms with the idea that someone wanted you dead, Scott imagined. If Spencer was terrified, who could blame him? No one spoke. There was only the low rattle of the engine running at reduced speed, and the occasional shouts from the other boats.

Concerned that Gwen might be watching them from the deck of the house and wondering what they were doing out here running around in circles, showing no interest in fishing, Scott decided to steer a slow course for Goose Island. They wove around the other small boats and headed south.

On one of the boats someone hooked a big one. Line played out, reeled in, played out. It went on for ten minutes, the clicking of nylon, fish fins splashing, shouts of encouragement from the other boats. Scott started back around Goose Island. A big cheer went up. The fisherman had landed a nice silver.

"How about it?" Scott said, trying to break the heavy mood that hung over them. "Shall we give it another try? Maybe we'll bring one in for dinner."

Jake nodded halfheartedly. Spencer looked at his pole and said nothing. Scott steered slowly back toward the other boats. The downrigger started to pull deep into the pools where the salmon fed. Scott frowned.

"What's the matter?" Jake said.

"I don't know. Feels funny. Not like usual. Should go straight down. It's angling."

"Seaweed?" Jake suggested.

"Maybe." It was difficult to explain. His old downrigger had been so perfectly balanced. He wondered if when he'd installed the new one he'd fouled up one of the lines. "I hate to louse up your fishing, but I think I'll just take a look. See what's binding her up." He hoped he hadn't caught one of the lines in the prop or the water intake valve.

Scott cut the engine, and while they rocked in the swells, he cranked the reel, watched the line that held the downrigger rise slowly toward the surface. Jake leaned over the stern to examine the grass under the transom.

"Hey, Doc," Jake shouted. "Come have a look."

Scott stopped cranking and bent over the transom to look where Jake pointed. It was a lump, much like grass, but smoother, no willowly strands like hair floating from it. Scott had seen something similar when he was in the navy, lumps like children's putty, taped to the hulls of ships by the frogmen. But it wasn't grass or moss or even putty. It was a highly explosive plastic, and somewhere it had a detonator, or someone waiting on shore to set it off.

17

"Explosives," Scott shouted. "Get down!"

Jake and Spencer hit the deck. Dandy looked startled.

"Down, boy!"

Scott quickly scanned the shore for the person who might be watching and waiting to set off the charge. He saw no one. Couldn't be sure. He started up the engine, steered the boat around so they were bow to shore, their faces more or less hidden in case someone was waiting to see, to be sure they were all on board before that person pressed the button that would set it off.

Scott checked on his passengers. On the floor by the stern seat, his face the color of paste, Spencer huddled beside Jake. He was hugging his arms, not talking or moving, frightened out of his wits.

"Should we abandon ship?" Jake asked from his kneeling position beside Spencer. Clearly Jake knew, as did Scott, that if the device were set to go off on a timer or if it were to be triggered by someone on shore, their only hope was to get in the water and swim like hell for the beach.

But, Scott reasoned, if it were on a timer, wouldn't it have blown by now? Same for shore detonation. What if it were set for speed or depth? This made no sense. They'd traveled up to fifteen knots coming out of Griffin Bay, and for the past twenty minutes they'd been circling over a tidal pool that dropped forty fathoms.

There was yet another problem to consider. If they abandoned ship, she'd blow right out here, and the other boats in her path would go with her. Scott's heart started to pound dizzily in his head. "You and Spencer swim for it. I'm going to stick. Maybe I can defuse it." If not, he could run the boat to the middle of the pass, at least make sure innocent people weren't killed.

Jake shook his head emphatically. "No way. If you're staying, so are we."

Scott wondered if Spencer agreed with this. But Spencer, crouched in the corner by the tackle box, his arms over his head, was in a state of speechless shock, incapable of decision. He wasn't going anywhere.

Scott leaned over the transom until his face brushed the water. Cupping his hands to shut out the rays of the sun, he took a closer look at the wad of gumlike substance sticking to the underside of the boat. Finally he was able to shut out the sunlight enough to see through the blue-green cloud of algae. Coming from the putty-like mass on the underside of the stern was a threadlike wire that ran through the water and tied into the downrigger line. His heart did another giant flip.

"What is it?" Jake said.

"Fulminating mercury fuse on the downrigger is a good guess. Set to detonate when it hits the air." Scott inhaled slowly. "If I had raised the downrigger another foot, we'd all be part of the landscape."

Jake nodded soberly. "Has to be detached underwater."

Unless there was another detonating device that would be set off when he touched the fuse, and a dozen other possibilities he didn't care to think about. Scott felt a deep chill. He kicked off his shoes.

"I can do this as well as you," Jake said.

"No! Need you up here. Keep Spencer on the floor. I'm going

101

to cut the engine. Try to keep the boat pointed to shore." He pulled off his shirt. "I've got to go in easy. Don't want to break that wire in case it's got another trigger."

This was ironic, considering that only moments ago they'd run around in circles, dragging their lines and undoubtedly come close to getting them tangled in the wire.

Dandy stood on the transom beside Jake and watched while Scott eased over the side and slipped feet first into the water. The icy cold moved up his legs to his chest, robbed him of breath. He waited a moment, then, inhaling deeply, went under.

It wasn't a steep dive. The wire was hooked into the downrigger just below the transom, and the downrigger was less than three feet from the surface. Three feet from death, Scott thought as he ran his hand gently over the lead ball. Could be a wire trigger. Easy does it.

He touched it. A plastic capsule the size and shape of a ball-point pen was taped to the lead ball. He worked quickly, telling himself his theory had to be right, a fulminating mercury fuse, a device that fit. He would have used it himself if he'd been intent on killing someone.

It didn't take long, holding his breath, less than a minute, undoing the wrap, using swift fingers usually used to explore muscles and tissues, but this wasn't a human belly. This was a dangerous detonating cap that, once fired, would blow them into a million pieces.

He didn't feel the cold as he worked unraveling the tape — only a few more seconds without air. He finally broke it free, ran his index finger over the ball again, didn't stop until he'd satisfied himself the surface was perfectly smooth as it was supposed to be. He was running out of wind, but he had one more thing to check.

He kicked and, holding the cap under the water, broke the surface, took a deep breath, and went down again. Holding onto the fuse, he swam, tracking the wire to the connector. Nothing. He traced it to the transom, ran his free hand over the gummy stuff plastered to the bottom of the boat. Then he discovered it. A second wire!

Just as he'd feared. Anyone who'd gone to so much trouble would have a backup plan. He let the fuse from the downrigger sink to the bottom. Encased in cold water, it would be forever safely buried in the mud and slime two hundred feet deep. Then he surfaced.

Jake and Dandy were leaning over the stern with anxious faces as Scott gulped in mouthfuls of air. Spencer didn't look up.

"Was it a mercury fuse?" Jake asked.

Scott nodded. "Set to go off when we pulled the downrigger out of the water."

"Sweet plan."

"I'm afraid that's not all of it. There's another wire coming out of the explosive. Goes off in a different direction."

"Uh-oh."

They were thinking the same. Another fuse somewhere on the boat and quite likely set on a timer.

Jake bit his lip in concentration. "Which direction?"

"Starboard, I think."

Wordlessly Jake began examining the gunwales from the stern to the cockpit along the starboard side. Scott swam around the big outboard, inspecting the hull along the waterline. Jake spotted it first, the barely visible wire on the antenna over the cockpit. Tucked neatly along the metal groove that braced the cockpit glass. It was taped under the gunwale. Scott swam back to the transom and boosted himself aboard.

"Timer?"

Jake nodded. "Give me that fish plier." His voice had an edge on it that said it might blow anytime.

Scott dumped the contents of the tackle box on the deck, grabbed the pliers, and placed them in Jake's outstretched hand.

"I think there's only one wire feeding it. I'm going to detach it."

Scott held his breath. "Go ahead."

He squeezed the pliers. The snap sounded like rifle fire on the silent deck. "Got it," he whispered.

"Set to go after the other was disconnected?"

"Uh-huh." Beads of perspiration formed on Jake's broad forehead. "It had four seconds left."

18

Jake's hands were steady on the crank as he raised the downrigger, but from the lines of stress on his face it was clear he was still unnerved. Spencer just sat there on the cabin floor, not moving or uttering a sound. Jake talked to him, much as he would a child, and finally Spencer stirred as though aroused from a deep sleep. There was, Scott thought as his old classmate blinked recognition at them, more wrong with him than could be answered by finding the person threatening his life.

Scott docked at the creek and sent Jake home in the Jeep with Spencer and Dandy. Then he ran the boat into the shipyard in Friday Harbor and called the sheriff. Speeding through the water, he thought only about getting the boat safely into the yard and hauled. But waiting for Leroy, he had what he imagined was a delayed reaction. As he sat on an oil drum in the shade of the boatshed writing his thoughts on a scrap of paper, his hands began trembling. He kept on writing, trying to assemble his ideas. By the time Leroy arrived, the shakes stopped, and he was breathing normally again.

The sheriff took immediate charge, supervised the boys working the lift while they positioned the sling under the small runabout, swung her gently out of the water, and dropped her on sawhorses. Then he dismissed the boatyard crew. "What they don't know they can't broadcast," he told Scott.

Water dripped on their heads from the boat's undersides as he and Scott examined the furry layer of grass growing from her bottom. Leroy bent under the hull and traced his finger over the plastic lump stuck to the transom. There was no fear of it exploding now without the charge, but Scott tensed up again at the reminder of how close they'd come to death.

Leroy shook his head solemnly. "Haven't seen anything like this since Vietnam."

"You know anything about explosives?"

Leroy leaned against the dolly. "Not enough. I think I'll call an expert. It'll tie up your boat for a few days, I'm afraid."

"No problem. I'm tired of fishing anyway."

As the absurdity struck him, Scott started to laugh. It was more out of relief than humor, but once started, he couldn't stop. He fell against the sides of the boat, the spasms bringing on tears. Finally, he choked an end to it and wiped his eyes. His chest was sore, and he felt foolish. "Sorry," he said.

Leroy's eyes were sympathetic. "I think you did well to get out of it alive."

"You think this was a professional job?"

Leroy removed his Stetson, set it on the sawhorse, and mopped the sweat off his temples. "Hard to say the way things are, with do-it-yourself bombs and all the nuts running loose."

Scott told him the rest of the story, about the air tank and what the shop people had said. "Why the devil didn't you tell me that yesterday?"

"I meant to, but I thought it was an accident, that there had to be another explanation. I tried to call you this morning, but you weren't in."

"Mmm," Leroy said, disapproval still in his voice. Then he asked questions. Who went on the dive? What equipment was used? His face registered its usual nonexpression, but Scott knew him well enough to read deep concern.

"What do you think?"

Leroy shook his head. "I hope the senator is smart enough to stay out of print on *this* one."

"Publicity is the last thing on his mind right now. It's finally dawned on him that someone really means to kill him, and he's plenty scared."

"Keep him that way."

"About protection . . ."

"I've already sent Harold out to the Cape." Leroy wiped his brow again, and from the deepening furrows on his forehead, Scott knew that in spite of his outward calm, he was worried. Two murders and an attempted assassination were all very much big-city stuff.

"I hate to ask, but do you suppose you could check a few things for me?" Scott presented Leroy with the list he'd jotted down while waiting for the boatyard people to haul the runabout.

Leroy looked at the list. "I dunno how cooperative Washington will be. Mmm. Do what I can. Frankly, Doc, my primary concern is keeping the senator alive until he leaves the island. After that, he's someone else's worry."

"You knew he was holding a reception at the house after the dig ceremony Friday?"

"That's what I mean about dumb."

Still unsettled, after Leroy left, Scott went in search of Vic. Vic had been in Special Services in the Korean War. He'd know something about bombs and the kind of people who planted them, and if Scott asked Vic to keep it quiet, Vic would do just that.

The *Nellie J* was tied up at the dock in Friday Harbor where she'd been since the blockade. Vic was on board, beer bottle in hand, puzzling over the little hen scratches in his notebook. He was organizing his search to discover who else had seen Red the day he was murdered. So far he'd had no luck. Scott told him about the bomb.

"I'll be damned. Somebody really wants to take the son of a bitch out. Mercury fuse, huh? And the backup on a timer?"

"Right."

"But only a single wire?"

"I figure he didn't have time to set up the second, which was mighty lucky for us."

Vic nodded. "You say you were away from the boat an hour?"

"At most."

106

"People hanging around the docks?"

"Didn't see a soul. Pretty quiet at that time."

"Uh-huh. He probably was counting on that. I'd look for someone with a military background or —"

Scott raised an eyebrow. "Or what?"

"Saw a bird in the service who had no special training, but he could wire anything. Smart. Read a lot."

"So who can we rule out?"

"No one. A kid could have done it."

Vic drove Scott back to the Cape in his big seventy-six Cadillac, steering with one finger on the wheel. He drove far too fast and talked continually about how Billy couldn't have killed Red, primarily because Vic knew him too well for that. He ignored completely the strong evidence against him. After the first couple of miles, Scott listened only sporadically, thinking about bombs and air tanks and crab boats. It all came down to motive and opportunity. Far too many had both.

With his preoccupations, Vic meandered all over the road. By the time they reached American Camp, Scott suggested mildly that they slow down so they could see the dig.

They rounded the turn by the yellowed grassland, and he dutifully eased up on the accelerator. All down the slope to Griffin Bay the students had carved more squares into the earth. The cuts generally were getting deeper and beginning to resemble a clay maze that ran very nearly to the edge of the tide flats.

An eagle soared overhead, scouring the banks where the rabbits had dug their tunnels. Nothing stirred on the grassy slopes. They left the dig and climbed the road around Mount Finlayson. Stretched out below them to the south was the lighthouse and Cattle Pass. Swirls of water tossed white foam in all directions. Changing of the tide. There were deep shadows on the water and a red glow over Fish Creek from the setting sun.

Al had hinted Erin might return soon. Too much to hope for. Still, it was such a thoroughly pleasant diversion, Scott smiled to himself over it. Vic continued talking and steering his reckless path past the lighthouse and the pillbox. His tires kicked up dust as they ran onto the graveled roads of the Cape.

"What do you think about that, Doc?" he said finally, presumably still talking about Billy.

"Umm," Scott said, unsure which particular aspect of Billy's case he had in mind.

"Yeah. My thoughts exactly," Vic said and laughed.

Leroy's deputy stopped them at the entrance to Scott's drive, poked his head in Vic's car window, saw Scott, and nodded. "Oh, hi, Doc. Just checking. Go on in."

"What the hell's that all about?" Vic said.

"Harold's here to protect Spencer."

"Turning your home into a goddamned fortress? You poor bastard."

Scott climbed out, and Vic threw the Cadillac into reverse, dug up gravel backing onto the road. "Yell if you need anything," he called. "Oh, by the way, they're giving us another day this week, so I'll be out trying to make a few bucks. You can catch me at night." With a grinning salute, he squirreled up the road, headed back toward town.

In the house, the mood wasn't so chipper. Gwen hadn't been told about the bomb or the air tank and wondered why Spencer had secluded himself in the bedroom after he returned from fishing.

Headache from too much sun, Jake had told her. "Saw no point in upsetting her," he confided to Scott.

Scott told him what Leroy had said about the importance of keeping it quiet, and Jake nodded agreement.

Gwen was sitting in the big leather chair with a book when Scott walked into the living room. She looked up, smiled a greeting, and then buried herself in the printed page again. Cliff downed a martini, his second, and walked out on the deck to stare moodily at the evening boat traffic going through the Pass.

Jake had called the Secret Service people and they'd promised to fly some agents over for the dig ceremony. "I tried my darnedest to talk the senator out of the whole thing," Jake said, confessing uneasiness. "I know he's scared, but he refuses to leave here until he's fulfilled his obligations."

"Is his reelection more important to him than his life?"

Jake scratched the tight black curls of his hair. "For a couple thousand voters on one small island, it doesn't make sense, does it?" Something else bothered Jake. "Doc, you've seen people come—well—unhinged by fear?"

"Saw a lot of it in the Vietnam vets."

"Exactly." Over toward Lopez Island, the dusk settled in over the trees. Jake's eyes watered. "Sometimes they stay that way."

"Spencer's always had a lot of resilience," Scott said cheerfully, trying to reassure the big man, who, in some strange way, appeared to blame himself for the problem.

Jake nodded doubtfully, and Scott didn't tell him his real clinical opinion, that he thought the incident on the boat had touched off a deep-seated emotional problem in Spencer and if another trauma occurred, he could come unhinged again, and as Jake said, this time perhaps he would stay that way.

With everyone in bad sorts that evening, Jake took over in the kitchen and revealed more of his hidden talents. He found some hamburger in the freezer and, with a can of mushrooms, sour cream, and red wine busied himself preparing dinner, humming as he worked.

"It's marvelous," Gwen said as they ate. "I must have the recipe."

"Poor man's stroganoff," Jake said, clearly pleased by her approval.

"You're a man of many surprises," Cliff said.

For Scott, however, the real surprise was Spencer. He rose from his nap, looking rested and alert. Over dinner he told stories about the dig and other archeological expeditions, about mastodons, and the early beginnings of the island—trying out Friday's speech, Scott guessed. He wove it all in with his political views, added a joke here and there, which provoked a smile even from Cliff. No one would have guessed that only a few hours earlier, Spencer had come a heartbeat from death or that he'd cowered on the floor of the small boat, too terrified even to speak.

After dinner, Gwen made coffee, and they sat in the living room and very quickly conversation went flat. Spencer sat limp in the big chair, worn out from the effort at dinner, and Cliff and Gwen joined him in a world of silence. Jake walked outside to get some air, and Scott yearned to get away from all of them.

That opportunity presented itself when Al walked in, followed by Harold. Dandy ran over to greet Chips, and Harold stood in the doorway with a question on his face. Did Al belong or not?

"What the heck's going on here?" Al said. "Since when do I need a police escort to see Scottie?"

Harold shrugged.

"Harold's our security guard," Scott explained. "Come on in, Al."

"Yes, by all means, come in, Professor. Have some coffee with us," Spencer called from the living room.

"Thanks. Can't stay. Just came to borrow a wrench. Kitchen drain's plugged."

"What a shame," Gwen said.

Scott went to look for the wrench. When he returned Al was giving Spencer some of his views on the dig, which were mainly negative. Spencer took it with good humor, and Scott left to go back to the house with Al and help him fix the drain.

"What was all that about with security guards?" Al asked as he and Scott walked back across the road, the dogs scampering ahead of them.

"It's a long story."

"I've got time."

On his hands and knees under the sink, Scott told Al about the bomb. Al threw his hands up in the air and let out a long sigh.

"Darned fool ought to go back to Washington before he gets somebody hurt."

Scott applied pressure on the wrench and the bolt loosened. Water spilled into the pail Al had set out for the purpose.

"I can take it from there," he said.

"Almost finished." Scott ran the snake up the drain and pulled out soap and a wad of hair. "Looks like you've been bathing Chips in the sink."

"Mmpf," Al said.

Scott finished the repair job, and they sat in the living room, drinking coffee and discussing the old man's theories about who might have wired the boat. Dusk settled over the water as they talked. As usual, Al favored the crime-of-passion theory, which pointed strongly to the women. Scott laughed at the idea.

In the middle of this, car lights flashed outside the window. Scott looked out through the trees to the drive. "Oh, hell."

"What's the matter?"

"Madelyn Ellis just drove in. She's probably here to tear the house apart again."

Al shook his head sympathetically. "Never mind. It'll all be over in a couple of days."

Scott nodded, cheered by the thought. "Say, you hear any more about when Erin's coming home?"

Al reached for his pipe from the top of a pile of books on his desk, grinning all the while. "Got a call just before dinner. She's flying in Monday for a week. Would you like to pick her up from the airport? She comes in on that late-afternoon flight from Seattle."

"Sure," Scott said, but his enthusiasm was gone. Coming for just a week, and she hadn't even let him know.

He was brooding over this when the door shook under a strong hand. Chips and Dandy started barking. Al got up to look. "Don't need to break the door down," he grumbled. "I'm coming."

It was Jake, and his face said there was more trouble. "It's Cliff, Doctor. On the beach. He's had a nasty fall. We were afraid to move him. I—I think he's still breathing."

19

Gwen was holding Cliff in her arms, splashing sea water on his head, when Jake and Scott reached the beach. Spencer watched. It was dark in the shadows of the rocky bank, but the light from the house exposed their faces enough for Scott to see that Cliff was fully conscious and that he wasn't wearing his glasses.

He looked up at Gwen and smiled feebly. Then he began groping around the sand and gravel. "Where are my glasses?"

Jake dropped to his knees and sifted through the sand, found the glasses by Cliff's foot. The frame was bent, but the glass, unbroken. Cliff put them on, tried to adjust them, gave up, stuck them in his shirt pocket, and ran his fingers lightly over his scalp. "Boy, does my head hurt."

Scott probed the dark thicket of hair and felt the lump that had formed over the crown. Cliff winced. The skin was broken and blood oozed from the wound. "Small hemotoma. You must have struck your head on the rocks when you fell."

"Fell? Who said I fell?" He'd been sitting on a log watching a seal that had surfaced outside the kelp bed, just watching and listening to the surf, he said, when he heard the sound of feet crunching on the rocks behind him. "I turned to look and someone hit me a good one. The lights went out, and that's all I remember."

Beside Scott, Spencer shuddered. "Someone struck you?"

"But why would anyone want to do that?" Gwen asked in a puzzled voice.

"Did you see who it was?" Jake asked.

"A man, I think. There was a boat—like a fishermen's skiff—not sure."

"That tears it." Harold moaned. "Leroy will kill me." But it had been Spencer the deputy had been sent to protect. How could he have expected anything to happen to Spencer's aide?

Scott looked across at Jake, wondering if he were thinking about Cliff being so like Spencer in size and build. In the dark it would be easy to mistake them. But Jake was standing with Al and the dogs on the mound overlooking Goose Island. A small boat laid a white trail toward the lighthouse. The boat's running lights were out, so except for the wake, it was only a dark shape racing through the inky waters of the Pass.

Harold started back up the bank to the house. "I'd better call Leroy."

Scott helped Cliff to his feet. "Feel dizzy or lightheaded?"

"A little woozy."

"Lean on me."

"I'm all right, Doc," he said, taking a step. He stumbled, grabbed Scott's arm, and allowed himself to be led up the bank and back into the house. He sank into the sofa and immediately complained of seeing double.

"You should go to the hospital," Scott said.

He shook his head. "Can't. There's the ceremony Friday and the media to deal with."

Gwen flashed her husband a concerned look. "This is ridiculous. Spencer can manage without you. Can't you, Spencer?"

From across the room, Spencer nodded absently. "If the doctor says you should go—go!"

"I feel fine," Cliff said meekly.

Scott proceeded to wash the sand out of the wound. "You could easily have a concussion. Hospital is the place for you, and no argument."

"They can fly you into Bellingham in twenty minutes," Al said.

"But we have a big day tomorrow, getting ready . . ." Concern was etched on his face.

"*Spencer* has a big day tomorrow," Scott said. "*You* have to rest."

Scott looked at Spencer for support, but Spencer was staring out the window into the night. Had he suddenly realized the very real possibility that Cliff hadn't been the intended victim at all?

Al called a local commercial pilot in Friday Harbor and arranged for the flight. "He'll pick you up at the creek in ten minutes."

Cliff nodded weakly. His eyes were dilated, and he was deathly pale in the lamp light, and Scott knew it had been the right decision.

Leroy arrived, followed by Robbie and Charleen, who said they'd been walking on the beach and saw the cars parked in front and stopped to see what was going on. Madelyn's husband, Dick, drove in shortly after, looking for his wife. Madelyn had come, she said, to go over last-minute arrangements for the reception.

Leroy patched in a call to his dispatcher to put out a Coast Guard alert for the boat. "Probably too late to do any good. A small boat like that can duck in anywhere. Unless, of course, you have a good description."

Jake and Al shook their heads. "Too dark."

Leroy sent Harold to the beach to check on footprints. Then he turned to Cliff. "What happened?"

Cliff went through it again, more coherently this time. He added a little about the sensation of being watched and of thinking he'd heard voices.

"Recognize any of them?"

Cliff shook his head.

Leroy asked Scott afterward if he thought a man knocked unconscious could hear anything.

"Maybe when he was coming out of it. Also, possibly he wasn't completely out."

"How long was he alone on the rocks?" Jake asked.

Harold answered. "He said he'd been there ten minutes before it happened."

114

"Who found him?"

"The senator's wife."

"Mmm," Leroy said.

Scott drove Cliff to the creek to meet the plane. Transporting patients to the mainland was routine for the pilot, who had already arranged for an ambulance to meet them in Bellingham. The color was returning to Cliff's cheeks, and Scott thought, Good, he's not in shock. Probably being overly conservative sending him to the hospital, but on the outside chance of brain damage, Scott wanted to be sure. "I still think I should fly over with you," Scott said. They'd argued about this on the ride to the creek.

"Forget it, Doc." Cliff grinned. "I'm fine." Then, turning serious again. "Besides, this makes it doubly important for you to keep a watch over the senator, don't you think?"

Leroy was still grilling everyone when Scott returned to the house. Madelyn said she'd arrived only moments before they found Cliff. She didn't remember seeing anything, but vaguely recalled hearing an outboard motor on the water.

"What about the neighbors?"

"Neighbors are all traveling right now," Al answered. "Scottie and I are the only ones around for a country mile."

Dick Ellis was visibly irritated at being detained and his resentment showed as he answered Leroy's questions. A flush rose from the edges of his neatly trimmed brown beard. "I haven't the slightest idea what any of it's about," the Friday Harbor attorney told Leroy. "I just got here. Haven't had my dinner yet." He shot Madelyn a dark look.

Madelyn ignored it.

"Did you see anything unusual when you drove in from the Cape road?"

"What would I see except the light from the lighthouse and the beacon off Iceberg Point?"

"What about boats? Sounds?"

"I just told you—nothing. Now, if you don't mind, I'd like to take my family home. I have early appointments tomorrow."

"They can go now, can't they, Sheriff?" Spencer said, coming up behind Ellis. "They've done a super job for me this week, and I don't want them dragged into something that doesn't concern them." Spencer draped one arm over Ellis and the other over Madelyn, and Ellis grew smiles all over his face. "You kids go home," Spencer said.

Leroy bit down. "Where's your son?"

"He doesn't know any more than I do," Ellis said.

Leroy gave him a hard stare. "I think I'll just discover that for myself, if you don't mind."

Robbie's grinning face appeared in the pass-through opening from the kitchen. "Here I am, Sheriff. Char and I were on the beach, but we didn't see anything."

"What about boats or anyone walking by the doctor's house?"

Charleen had been in the kitchen pouring herself a glass of water. On the question, she slipped in behind Robbie and wrapped her long arms around his neck so it looked as though he'd grown another pair. "Saw a boat going up San Juan Channel. One of the fishing boats, I think."

"North or south?"

"North," Robbie said.

"South by the lighthouse," Charleen said, laughing.

"Which is it?"

Robbie shrugged.

"See anyone on the beach before that?"

"We were a little preoccupied."

Charleen giggled, and, looking annoyed, Leroy gave up.

Harold didn't find anything on the beach. "There are footprints, sure, but without a scorecard, how could you tell who they belong to or when they were made?"

Dick Ellis shook his head irritably. "I'm heading for home," he said to his wife. "You coming?"

"Be right behind you." This time Madelyn said her good-byes to Spencer with a clutching of hands. "Don't worry," she called to Scott as she started toward her car. "My committee will be here bright and early Thursday to get the house ready for the reception."

"Terrific," Scott said unenthusiastically.

After they left, Leroy speculated about what weapon the attacker might have used.

"Piece of driftwood, perhaps," Scott said. "It was only a small contusion."

"Could he have been killed by the blow?"

"Wrong place for it. If it had struck the temporal region, and if it had been — well — a harder blow, it could've been a different story."

Robbie and Charleen were the last to leave. Robbie thought he could take over some of Cliff's jobs on publicity, and while he and Spencer discussed this, Charleen said to Scott, "I hear Billy Leroux is a friend of yours."

"Yes, he is."

"Do you think it's fair what they're doing to him?"

"I know Billy is innocent," Scott said warily.

She nodded enthusiastically. "Do you think he might not get a fair hearing because he's Indian?"

"No. Leroy's a fair man."

"Is the senator helping?" There was sarcasm in her voice.

"There isn't much he can do."

"But Billy needs help. Right?"

"Well — yes —" He wondered at the direction of her thoughts.

She touched his arm lightly. "That's what we thought."

Scott started to ask who *we* was and what she had in mind, but Robbie returned to claim her and whisked her out the door with the question still on Scott's lips.

20

Cliff called the following day to report he was doing well and expected to return for the dedication. Spencer shut himself in the den to work on his speech, and Gwen and Scott passed the day sunbathing and walking the beach. Jake went into hibernation with a book.

Thursday morning early, as promised, Madelyn and the women arrived to prepare the house for the reception. Gwen helped, and Scott went back to the beach. This time Jake joined him. Tomorrow couldn't come soon enough, Jake said, because the next day they'd be flying home.

No one talked much at breakfast Friday. Spencer drank coffee while he read over the notes for his speech. Cliff arrived early, pale-faced but eager to help. Gwen fussed over him, and Spencer put him to work on press handouts.

Scott left Jake and Cliff to deal with getting Spencer and Gwen safely to the dig for the ceremony, which was to begin at eleven. Then he picked up Al and drove them to the spot where the weekend celebrations were to begin.

A gull floated over the sun-baked clay trenches below American Camp as he parked the Jeep. In front of the makeshift platform that had been set up for the ceremony was a wooden pig from which Spencer would later deliver his address. A number of students carrying signs were parading back and forth in front of it. The Seattle television crews were there, too, catching the whole thing.

Scott frowned. He hadn't even thought about demonstrations.

"Kids! Give 'em the world and it's not enough," Al said as he shuffled alongside Scott down the yellowed slopes toward Griffin Bay and the site of the dig. The mid-morning sun beat down on the large stretch of open field. It was already hot, and Al was beginning to look a little wilted.

As they approached the perimeters of the cuts where the dried grass turned into dirt, Scott was able to make out the signs. "Equal Rights for Indians." Some were addressed to "Senator Manning."

"I'm afraid it's about Billy," Scott said.

Al wiped sweat off his narrow brow with a large white handkerchief and shook his head. "That's all poor Billy needs. A bunch of nuts biasing a jury."

Scott was afraid it was the least of Billy's concerns, but didn't comment.

The students carried other signs, demanding increased funding for the dig, which drew more grumbles from Al. But it wasn't the content of the signs that bothered Scott. It was their contribution to an atmosphere of uncertainty.

Well below the dig, overlooking Griffin Bay, a stand had been set up on the grass facing the platform. A few townspeople and tourists had already begun filling up the seats. Scott headed for the front row and ran into Charleen, holding one of the signs. "I told you we'd help," she said.

Scott smiled back at her. "Yes, you did. I'm sure Billy will appreciate your efforts."

"We're doing our best."

"I know you are, and I'm certain you won't let it get out of hand."

Impulsively she dropped her sign and gave Scott a hug. "You

119

can count on it, Dr. Eason." Her cheeks were flushed and her eyes fired with excitement as she left them to rejoin her friends.

"Mmpf. Crazy as her mother."

"Her mother?"

"I told you. Holly's child. Committed suicide. Remember?"

"But her name's Johnson."

"Her maternal grandmother's name. Grandmother raised the girl. She took her name."

As Charleen trudged across the dusty field, a slender figure in sweats and jeans, Scott thought about Holly and Spencer that summer and about Robbie and Holly's daughter. "Poor kid," Scott murmured.

Spencer's limousine rolled in ten minutes late. Spencer and Gwen drew a trickle of applause as Jake and Leroy led them to their places on the platform. Cliff followed. Eyes riveted on Gwen, who was wearing a brilliant blue silk dress that showed off everything to advantage. Spencer wore a pale-gray suit and a red tie, and his face had the flush of television makeup. Two men standing near the platform paid no attention to either of them but kept their eyes on the audience. Scott guessed they were Secret Service.

They opened the ceremony with the flag salute. Then a local girl, accompanied by the high school band, sang "The Star Spangled Banner." The chairman of the Pig War committee gave a brief history of the boundary dispute that had existed between the United States and Canada over the shooting of a San Juan Island pig. There was some friendly joking between officials of both governments and, finally, the mayor of Friday Harbor introduced Spencer.

The student demonstrators had been quiet through these preliminaries, and Scott was hopeful they would remain so, but when Spencer walked over to the wooden pig and mounted the steps, they began marching around it, chanting "Free Billy." It was just the sort of distraction Scott had feared. Spencer flashed the big grin. He had no time to do anything else. The boom came right out of the hillside. It rocked the stands. For a split second the field was paralyzed into hollow silence. A second blast shattered the air all across Griffin Bay. From behind the platform, a black smoke cloud rose into the air.

Scott couldn't see Spencer any longer, but on stage behind the pig, Leroy was on his feet, gun out, searching the crowd. Scott started for the wooden pig. Secret Service men scrambled out the aisles. There must have been a dozen of them. They ran onto the field in a race to reach Spencer. A woman screamed. Someone shouted, "Terrorists!" It started a stampede for the road.

Jake and Scott and two Secret Service men reached Spencer at the same time. They found him crouched on the floor by the pig, covering his head as he had in the boat the day before. Around the edges of the makeup, his face was ghostly white. He opened his mouth to speak, but no words came out.

"He's been shot," Cliff gasped, coming up behind Gwen.

"No," Jake said.

Jake and Scott pulled Spencer to his feet while the Secret Service men crawled around the pig, probably looking for more bombs. Leroy ran over with Gwen. Robbie burst out of nowhere, ran ahead to the limousine, and held the car door open.

"Get them out of here," Leroy shouted.

With Jake on one side and Cliff on the other, they ran Spencer and Gwen to the waiting car, loaded them both into the back. Robbie slammed the door shut. Jake jumped into the driver's seat and, without so much as a blink, threw the car into gear and raced up the road, kicking up a thick cloud of dust behind them.

Scott looked for Robbie, but he and Charleen were making a fast track for the parking lot. Scott rushed back to Al. The old man was still in his seat, watching the confusion in the field. People scurried up the hill to their cars. The platform was empty. On the field, racing around like hounds on scent, the Secret Service men searched the grounds.

Scott sniffed the air. It smelled of rotten eggs. "A cherry bomb!"

Al nodded, and they started across the field. "Did you see our senator dive for cover? Scared the liver out of him."

"I think that's what it was intended to do."

21

Leroy ended the bomb scare. "Couple kids with firecrackers," he told Scott and the others standing on Scott's deck in the sun.

Inside, the house brimmed over with guests. Madelyn had put vases of cut flowers everywhere. The sweet scent of roses wafted through the rooms as the reception went on in spite of the unsuccessful conclusion to the dedication ceremony.

"A ten-year-old and his eight-year-old brother," Leroy said wearily.

"What are you doing with them?" Al asked.

Leroy shrugged. "What do you do with kids that age except try to scare them? They had no idea what kind of furor it would cause. They thought it was a joke."

"I'll bet someone put them up to it," Dick Ellis said.

"Ought to put them in jail," someone else said.

Leroy shook his head and walked into the living room. Scott and Al followed. Spencer stood in the middle of a crowd of local politicians. Except for the highball he held in his hand, by Scott's count his third, he appeared normal, laughing it off with the rest of the guests. But with the story certain to highlight the evening news, it had to be an embarrassment.

Al positioned himself by the punch bowl and helped himself to the champagne. Madelyn had put on a tape with some soft elevator music, and she and her committee people were making every effort to give the appearance that Spencer's visit to the island was a political triumph.

"Isn't it amazing how people flock to see a celebrity?" Al said.

Scott observed the growing number of strangers still coming into the house, and a chill came over him. Then he spotted Jake and Leroy hanging around Spencer like glue and a couple of the Secret Service men circulating between. The chill passed.

"Where's your big chair?" Al said, doffing his cup at the spot near the fireplace now taken up by people.

Scott sighed. "Madelyn must have moved it again."

Al shook his head sympathetically and then, spotting an old friend from the Island Historical Society, excused himself.

Scott sought out Gwen, wondering how she was doing after the bomb scare. She was in the kitchen filling a cookie tray and taking the incident pretty much in stride. Clearly she still hadn't been told about the attempts on Spencer's life, and so thought everyone had overreacted. "You have to expect these things when you're in politics. Confidentially, though," she whispered, "if I found the little bastards who did it, I'd wring their necks. It scared Spencer out of ten years of his life."

"What about you?"

She laughed. "I grew up with younger brothers."

Madelyn rushed in and deposited an empty tray on the counter, took the full one from Gwen. "Hurry up with those dishes," she snapped to Nancy, who had her elbows deep in dishwater.

"Right away," Nancy said good naturedly.

In the living room, Madelyn's helpers worked feverishly filling up the coffee urns and refilling the punch bowls. Watching all the activity, Gwen got a sudden attack of conscience. "Got to go," she told Scott, and left to meet more of Spencer's supporters.

Left alone, Scott wandered onto the deck and found a quiet spot on the corner. Dandy, who'd been lying on the cool grass under the deck, loped up the stairs toward him, miraculously not bumping a single leg or elbow on his way up.

123

Scott and the dog sat together on the deck rail. The small pleasure boats were coming in for the late-afternoon salmon run. The wavelets bounced them around, and there was much laughing and yelling back and forth. Scott thought, Two kids with cherry bombs? And three weeks to the fourth of July. It didn't jibe.

A slight breeze came up on the water and splashed over onto the deck, cooling it pleasantly. Just below the deck, angry voices carried up with the wind.

"I can't believe you did anything so stupid."

"They were jobs to be done, and I did them."

"Without questioning? Come on."

"You're making a big deal out of it."

A deep feminine sigh. "You're an idiot!"

The voices faded, and a few moments later Robbie and Charleen walked onto the deck from the other side and went to join Spencer in the living room. Robbie looked glum, but Charleen was smiling. She did, in fact, look so different in every respect that Scott barely recognized her.

She'd fixed up her hair, for one thing. It fell in soft waves over her bare brown shoulders instead of hanging straight. She'd added color to her lips and accented her pale-brown eyes, for another. And she wasn't wearing jeans. She had on a bright-red sundress, which she filled out nicely. There was absolutely nothing to identify her as the girl who'd demonstrated earlier — a good thing, considering.

Spencer went through his usual routine, holding her hand, the intimate smile. Robbie left. Charleen stayed. She was a beautiful young girl in bloom, a fact that didn't go unnoticed by Spencer, who eyed her as if it were for the first time, which, in a sense, was probably the case. They talked for a moment and then walked onto the patio, still talking.

In the living room, Madelyn watched with a frown. From the kitchen door, Gwen also observed. Scott started to say something to Gwen, but there was a strange expression on her face he couldn't quite identify. She retreated into the kitchen, and Scott said nothing.

As the afternoon sun shifted to the west and left the deck in shadows, most of the guests wandered back to the living room. Scott stayed on the deck. Dick Ellis joined him. He planted a sandaled foot on the rail and talked companionably about the dig ceremony, blaming the mayor and his "small-town mentality" for the problems. He would have arranged it all differently, he said.

Scott quickly got the idea Ellis enjoyed the prestige that came from his association with Spencer, and if he minded his wife and son putting in overtime on Spencer's behalf, he hid it well. Spencer had him appointed regional head of Legal Services. Next, Ellis anticipated a federal judgeship. There were business ventures, too. Stroking his beard, he said, "I guess I don't need to tell you it pays to have friends in high places."

Scott smiled, remembering when Spencer had offered him an appointment to the Medicare Screening Board and Scott had shocked Spencer by turning it down. The job went to Joe Dearborn, an internist Scott knew who'd contributed heavily to Spencer's campaign. Joe liked to talk about his business deals with Spencer, too. Funny, though, last time Scott had run into him, Joe hadn't said a word about it.

Ellis drained his punch cup. He looked at his watch and then into the living room where Madelyn was talking to Spencer. For a fraction of a second his smile fizzled. Then it flashed on again. "Well—guess I should get Madelyn to wind down. Been good talking to you, Doctor." He saluted with his empty cup and returned to the living room with a little droop to his shoulders.

As dusk spread its dark shadows on both sides of the house, the commercial fishermen started rumbling around the point. They blasted their horns and waved as they powered past the house. Scott waved back. They weaved around the small pleasure boats, throwing giant white plumes of water behind, and steered a sure course through the shoal passage by Goose Island, headed to the strait.

Tonight it was the gillnetters and bow pickers. By morning the purse seiners would have their turn, and Vic would go out on the

Nellie J. Tomorrow this whole silly business would be over. Monday Erin would be home. Scott released a happy sigh. The guests started to leave.

In front of the deck a late flock of terns beat a ribboned trail over the water and exploded into the air. The party guests headed for their cars. The Secret Service people withdrew to their own vehicles, presumably to keep a night watch from the road. Jake and Leroy briefed Scott on the security measures for the remaining hours of Spencer's visit. They would post men on the road and the drive. Not much sleep for any of them.

Al walked over to say good night. With much hugging and laughing, Madelyn finally bade her farewells to Spencer and Gwen. She kissed Spencer and then, without prejudice, bussed Gwen as well.

"I'll fly back there next month," Madelyn said. Then to Scott, "Do you mind if we finish the cleanup in the morning?"

"Fine," Scott said.

When the last guest was out the door, Spencer fell onto the sofa. "Ahh," he sighed. He looked as drained as an actor after the last curtain. "If it won't offend any of you," he said, "I think I'm going to bed."

"Good idea, dear," Gwen said. "I'll join you in a few minutes."

There were deep tired lines on Spencer's face, and Scott thought what a disappointment it all must have been and in only a few weeks' time he would have to return to the state to campaign. Scott felt a sudden surge of sympathy for his old classmate. "Get some rest," he said.

Outside on the small pleasure boats, the skippers reeled in their lines and began heading for home, leaving the serious fishing to the commercials. By Goose Island the moon cast a golden trail over the water. There wasn't a ripple on the pass all the way to Deadman Island and beyond.

Scott carried his leather chair back into the living room, and Gwen made a pot of coffee. For the next couple of hours, Scott sat with Jake, Cliff, and Gwen, chatting about the events of recent days. A few minutes after midnight, Jake complained of being sleepy and retired to the bunk room. Cliff followed shortly.

Gwen leaned back on the sofa and gazed out at the sliver of light on the water. A dark cloud moved in behind the moon.

"Could rain," Scott observed.

"It's so beautiful," she said, and then, looking straight at him, "I hate to leave."

"I hate to see you go." Gwen had been a welcome relief these past days, lightened it for all of them. She was a pleasant companion, a good sport, and he'd have to be blind not to notice she was also an extremely attractive woman. He would miss her.

She walked over to his chair and perched on the edge beside him. The sweet scent of her perfume made him a little lightheaded.

"Scottie," she murmured, leaning over him so closely her hair brushed his cheeks and he felt the soft pressure of her bosom against his shoulder. "This has been a marvelous vacation for me because of you. You've been wonderful." She began stroking his arm.

Her lips were dangerously close. "Ummm, you must come again soon," he said.

Her dark eyes sparkled humor as she bent her head over his and kissed him. Her lips were soft and she smelled sweet. He got a prickly sensation in his chest that moved down his groin. She allowed her hand to slide gently to his knee. The tingling traveled to his toes. It all spelled deep trouble. He didn't return the kiss. He didn't resist it, either. He didn't move. He didn't even breathe.

From the water, an engine started up. Her lips lingered, half-parted, inviting participation. He thought about Spencer alone in the next room and did nothing. Finally, slowly, she moved away. "Good night, Scottie," she said. Then, stroking his arm a last time, "Spencer is fortunate to have such a good friend."

As he watched her leave to join her husband in bed, he didn't feel like a good friend at all. He sat in the chair for several minutes after she left, waiting for the pulsating sensations to stop and reflecting on her relationship with Spencer. Neglected, alone much of the time. As he tasted the traces of her lipstick, he felt a good deal of guilt.

Tired, he began turning out lights. The only sound in the house was Jake's peaceful snoring from the bunk room. Now the security guards were posted outside, Scott imagined it was the first night in days the big man had allowed himself a full night's sleep.

Through the window in the living room, headlamps flashed. Looked like Leroy's wagon turning into the drive. Scott wandered barefoot outside, hoping the sheriff's return didn't mean more trouble. It started to rain, and out on the lawn, Leroy conferred with his deputies.

"Oh, hi, Doc," Leroy said.

"Anything wrong?"

"I'm putting on extra men."

Scott got an unpleasant feeling. "Why?"

Leroy sighed. "Just talked to the Secret Service people. You know how these federal boys are. Don't want to tell you a darned thing, if they can help it."

"Tell you what? That was only a harmless prank out there today, right?"

"The kids and the firecracker, sure. But they dug around afterward and found a real bomb, with a timer. Same deal as your boat. And believe me, Doc, it wasn't the kids who planted that one."

Scott's whole body went numb. "Where?"

"Under the floor of the wooden pig. They'd checked it out before the ceremony, too, but whoever did it was a real pro. You could say the senator owes those kids his life. If the senator had stuck around another fifteen minutes, he'd have been blown to kingdom come."

22

It was still dark when Scott felt a cool hand on his bare chest. He jumped awake and stared into Gwen's worried face.

"It's Spencer," she said. "He's gone."

Scott propped himself up on one elbow and looked through blurry eyes at the clock on his nightstand. It was four-thirty. Outside, the gulls were crying before the first light. "He must have gone for a walk."

Gwen shook her head. "He hasn't been in bed for the past two hours. It rained last night, and his jacket's still on the chair. He wouldn't have gone without it. Even if he had, he'd be back by now."

Scott sat up. "You search the house?"

She nodded. "I woke about two, and he wasn't there. I thought he'd just gone to the bathroom. I—I must've fallen asleep again. When I woke the next time it was three-thirty, and he still wasn't there. I got up, looked around, went back to bed. Scott, I'm worried."

He could see from her eyes that she was.

"He has a blood pressure problem, you know."

Scott reached for his pants on the chair. "Go wake Jake."

Jake was up like a shot and ran to the beach in his briefs. Cliff, still in pajamas, ran after him. They returned shortly to report there was no one in sight anywhere, and since it was high tide, it was impossible to tell if anyone had been there.

Scott called Leroy and then went to get Harold while Jake dressed. Harold called in the Secret Service men, who'd been on watch outside all night. The limousine was still in the drive.

The Secret Service people had seen no one.

Gwen screwed her face up as though she might break into tears. "Then where is he? This isn't like him. It isn't like him at all."

"Probably gone for a walk on the beach," Cliff said, trying to console her.

Jake and Scott exchanged worried glances.

"Let's split up and look for him," Scott suggested.

Jake and Cliff started out, walking north toward the cave. Harold drove with the Secret Service men to the lighthouse. From the road, they would fan out to Eagle Cove and back around by Fish Creek. The sun was just peeking over Mount Baker as Scott started out on foot toward the lighthouse by way of the beach. Maybe Spencer had stopped to watch the sunrise from the sand flats. Sitting on a log, he'd be hidden by the road.

With Dandy at his side, Scott ran down the beach, kicking at driftwood and exploring the brush where the bank rose onto the grass. He looked out to Goose Island, thinking maybe Spencer had found a boat and rowed out, but there were only the rocklike clumps of seals wiggling awake.

Shortly, Leroy arrived, and he and Scott and the Secret Service people compared notes. In all their searchings from Eagle Cove to Fish Creek and Griffin Bay, there'd been no sign of Spencer. Leroy called his office in Friday Harbor and snapped instructions to his boat patrol, told his dispatcher to have the Coast Guard conduct a body hunt, which amounted to dragging the sea along the shoreline. Deep waters, of course, would be a waste of time.

Leroy put the phone down and saw the alarm written on Gwen's face. Cliff glared at him and the big man got all flustered. "It's just routine," he said. "Seldom comes to anything."

Gwen's lips quivered as she turned to the sink and started filling the coffeepot.

Scott and Jake were discussing where they should look next when Al and Chips walked in. Scott told him Spencer was missing.

"Probably went for a walk and got himself lost on Mount Finlayson," Al said.

Gwen's face brightened. "Do you really think so?"

"Good possibility," Al said, more optimistically than Scott thought wise.

The woods on Mount Finlayson were home to the deer, small animals, and the Cape's water supply, but hardly a place where a person would wander at night. Gwen was hopeful, so, more for her sake than out of conviction they'd find Spencer there, Scott said he and Al would check it out.

"I'll go, too," she said.

Scott shook his head. "No—better for you to stay here, in case something comes up." He didn't want Gwen there if they found Spencer. Cliff decided to stay with Gwen and handle any calls that might come in.

Leroy approved the search in the woods. "If you run into anything, yell."

Al and Scott loaded the dogs into the Jeep, and leaving Leroy to continue the search around the house, they started out. They bounced all over the seats as Scott sped over the rutted roads, past the lighthouse. He drove right by the lower wood road and on up to the rise in the land where the big firs stood swept back by the wind at the crest of the mountain.

"You missed the road," Al pointed out.

Scott nodded. "It'll be pretty dark in there yet. We wouldn't see much. Anyway, I want to play a hunch. Hang on."

Scott veered off the road and struck out across the dunes. They banged over the sand and crabgrass, hitting bumps and rocks. Al hung onto the door bar for dear life. The dogs slipped all over the backseat. They raced along the edge of the cliff, stopped by a big

131

rock, got out, and walked over to a grass ledge. Down the boul-
dered cliffs, the waves pounded the rocks that reefed out to sea.

"I know what you're thinking," Al said as they surveyed the
treacherous drop-off. "But if he fell, you're not going to know
about it until low tide."

Scott felt a new anxiousness. "Let's go on to American Camp."
He rammed the Jeep into gear, and they took off again over the
dunes. This time Dandy and Chips positioned themselves against
the bumpy ride and lay flat on the seat. Al held onto the door bar
again and stared straight ahead as they rattled across the lumpy
rolls of grass, missed the peat bog, passing thickets of ash trees
and wild roses.

The front tires bounced over an outcropping of rocks. They
flew over a clump of grass and slammed back down onto hard
clay, jarred every spur in Scott's spine. He thought about Spencer
with a potential heart problem and didn't slow down. They hit
another bump, and Chips flew over the seat into Al's lap.

Al let out an uncharacteristic "Damn! Scottie, slow down."

"Sorry." Scott eased on the accelerator, and they continued until
they reached the flagpole and the site of American Camp. The
dogs ran around the patches of green grass by the ranger's house.
Scott and Al followed them to the ridge. Below them lay the ice-
blue waters of the Strait of Juan de Fuca. Capping waves gleamed
white in the early-morning sun. Across the vast fetch of water,
the Olympic Mountains rose in sharp teethlike peaks against the
pale-blue sky. It seemed so out of place, the idea that even as they
stood there, Spencer might already be dead.

"Nothing down here," Al said.

"Let's try South Beach."

"I thought you said the sheriff's men had already checked
there."

Scott shrugged. "No harm in giving another look."

He parked the Jeep behind a log boom, and on foot, they followed the dogs over the west driftwood until they reached the
sand. White frothy combers ran over the beach for miles. There

was only the cry of the gulls and the crashing of the surf to break the morning's silence, and no one on the beach as far as they could see.

"I don't think this is getting us anywhere," Al said.

Scott agreed. "Let's circle back to the dig and check out Griffin Bay. If there's nothing there, then we can drive into the woods. By then it should be light enough to see something."

It was only a short drive to the road overlooking the dig. Scott parked the Jeep, and they walked again.

The sun was beginning to warm up the hillside, drying everything out from the rain the night before. Off to the west, a young doe grazed. The dogs lit out after it, and the deer darted into the woods. Scott called the dogs back. After a lot of yelling and whining, the dogs returned, and they trudged on to the edge of the dig not far from where they'd walked the morning before. The dogs raced ahead, noses to the ground. All across the field for a couple hundred yards, the bare earth lay exposed in neatly tiered rows. From Al's expression, Scott thought it was the first time the old man had really looked at what the students had done here. His face said he was impressed.

"Shall we just walk down to the stands and check out the cuts? It's always possible Spencer could've fallen into one of the holes and broken his leg, or had a heart attack." Scott really didn't think it likely, but as he had no other ideas, and they already were here, it seemed logical to check it out.

"Did he have too much to drink last night?" Al asked.

"Didn't seem to."

"Mmpf," Al said grumpily.

Dandy and Chips were well ahead of them, rooting up bits of grass.

"Rabbits," Al said, chuckling at the sight of the big sheepdog and his small fluffy companion racing across the field together.

Scott and Al followed. Occasionally Al gave a grudging nod of approval at the carefully chiseled cuts. "Must have a new man on it."

At the lower end of the dig, the dogs were all worked up about something. Remembering the fight Dandy had gotten into with a raccoon last summer, which resulted in the dog requiring several stitches in his ear, Scott ran on ahead. "Better see what they've trapped."

"Probably just a wood rat."

Scott checked out the holes as he ran. They were all puddled up from last night's rain. When he reached the dogs he nearly fell over Dandy, who had his eyes on Chips. Chips was sitting in the middle of one of the holes, his white hair dripping water and mud. "Chips, you're a mess."

Then Scott saw the toe of a shoe sticking up out of the murky water and the head half covered with it. "Over here, Al," Scott said grimly.

Al joined him, and they both looked down into the hole. There, lying face up in the pool of muddy water, was Spencer Manning, and clearly he'd been there much too long.

23

Below them in Griffin Bay, the seagulls squalled over scraps from the fish buyer's barge. The earth smelled of sour clay and wet grass. Al and Scott stared solemnly into the ditch, the morning mist falling heavy all around them.

"He looks so peaceful," Al said, shaking his head.

Scott stepped into the hole, waded in mud, and felt for the pulse, but he knew Spencer was dead, that he probably had been for a couple of hours. He'd never been a close friend. Most of the time, Scott hadn't liked him much, but seeing his old classmate lying in the mud hole, dead long ahead of his time, Scott felt deep pangs of regret. Somehow, he should have been able to prevent it. "Damn," he murmured. "Damn."

"Murder?" Al said.

It was such a strange question. Scott hadn't even considered natural causes, yet from the serene expression on Spencer's mud-streaked face, it was hard to believe he'd met a violent end. "I'd better get Leroy. Can you stay with him?"

Al nodded. "But don't take too long."

Scott found Leroy in his patrol car, coming out of Scott's drive. On the news, Leroy slapped the car wheel with the flat of his hand. "Oh, hell!"

Postponing the dreaded job of telling Gwen, Scott led Leroy back to the spot.

"Looks like he just fell asleep," Leroy said. "What do you think killed him?"

"I haven't examined him." Scott crouched down in the mud and ran his hand over Spencer's skin. It was cool and firm to the touch. He probed for several minutes, looking for a sign of violence. No bullets, no scratches or bruises, no needle tracks, no rope or wire marks. Scott shook his head at Leroy. "Can't tell without lab work, but just to look at him, I'd say a coronary." He studied Spencer's face, so fully relaxed. "Or . . ."

Leroy caught the hesitation. "Or what?"

Scott shrugged. "Drug overdose cases have much the same look, as though they've gone into a permanent sleep."

"Cocaine?"

Scott nodded. "But it doesn't figure."

"Why not?"

"I just don't see Spencer as a user. Anyway, he was far too ambitious to ruin his career with drugs."

Leroy began walking around the hole, studying the ground. "Why did he come all the way out here?"

"Maybe he was meeting someone," Al suggested.

Leroy frowned. "How did he get past my men?" He stepped into the hole and ran his hands along the sides and bottom of the mud pool. He stepped out and paced a twenty-foot area around the hole. "No signs of a struggle. No prints, either."

135

"Wouldn't the rain have washed any prints away?"

Leroy nodded. "And the grass is so hard, wouldn't be any there. I'll get a crew on it. There has to be something."

Scott was still going over Spencer's body. "Curious."

"What is?"

"These little impressions on the skin."

Leroy knelt beside him and looked. "Don't see anything."

"They're very faint, little waffle-iron marks."

The sheriff looked again. "Ummm. Well, let's call the Secret Service boys. They'll probably want to send the body to Seattle. They'll bring the King County coroner in on this one."

It was the first reference to the fact that Spencer was an important public figure and his death commanded special attention. The three of them looked at each other glumly as the full realization of what that meant struck them. The eyes of an entire nation would now be focused on San Juan Island. Leroy let out a long sigh. "Let's get on with it."

The Secret Service got Leroy's call in their car and arrived in less than five minutes. They made the expected decision to fly the body into Seattle without delay and called their own team in to examine the site. Al suggested Spencer's wife might have something to say about moving him.

Gwen! Scott had almost forgotten.

"We'd better talk to her," one of the Secret Service men conceded.

Scott left them making arrangements from their car phones, and he and Al raced back to the house in the Jeep. Scott didn't want Gwen hearing about Spencer from a stranger. It also occurred to him as he sped back toward the lighthouse that as soon as that call went out to the coroner, the media would know. He most definitely didn't want Gwen to learn of her husband's death from the morning news.

When he reached the house, he sat beside Al in the Jeep for a moment, his hand on the door handle, thinking how he should break it to her.

"Tough job," Al said sympathetically.

Not as though he hadn't had this unhappy task before. "Yeah. Better get it over with."

Jake and Gwen were waiting for him. Cliff was on the phone in the den. The sun poured in from the big living-room windows and caught the worried lines on Gwen's face. "You found him?" she said in an uncertain voice.

Scott had never found an easy way to say it. Direct, straight out usually worked best. "I'm sorry, Gwen," he said softly. "Spencer's dead. Looks like a coronary."

She went milk white and fell against Jake.

"Heart attack?" Jake said in disbelief.

"Won't know for sure until we get the lab reports back, but it looks that way."

"Where did you find him?"

"At the dig."

The big man frowned, and Scott knew what he was thinking. Spencer wouldn't have gone there in the middle of the night — not voluntarily.

But Gwen didn't question this. "All that way?" she said in a faraway voice. Then, burying her face in Jake's chest, she began to weep.

Cliff came in on this, took one look at them, and understood. He fell into a chair. Tears formed in his eyes. He looked like a light that had just gone out.

Word of Spencer's death spread swiftly. The media descended on the Cape. The death of a United States senator was headline news. They cluttered up the Cape roads and Scott's drive, photographed the house from every angle. It was Scott's worst nightmare come true and Cliff, still in a state of shock, seemed unable to deal with it.

Leroy posted deputies around the house to keep the reporters off the deck, but this proved ineffective against the resourcefulness of the media people. A network cameraman climbed one of the big firs on the neighbor's property, and with his zoom lens caught

137

Gwen slumped in the big living-room chair holding a whiskey and soda, which Scott had prescribed to settle her nerves. It was hardly the image she wanted to project on the national news.

Jake spotted the reporter from the deck and raced across the lawn like a madman. He caught the reporter by the leg, pulled him to the ground, grabbed his camera, and was about to smash it over the man's head when Scott and one of Leroy's deputies got there to stop him.

"Cool it," Scott said, and Jake let the man go.

The reporter ran back to the road, throwing threats of lawsuit over his shoulder. Jake watched, still smoldering with anger.

"That temper could get you into big trouble," the deputy warned sternly.

By lunchtime Cliff had recovered enough to perform his duties, which he did quite capably. The media left them alone.

In the afternoon, Gwen had a procession of well-wishers. Madelyn and Dick Ellis and Robbie were among the first. Robbie looked grim. Madelyn's eyes were swollen and red, and for once, she allowed her husband to do all the talking.

"Sorry, Gwen," Ellis said. "If you need any legal advice, you know I'll be only too happy to . . ."

"Thank you," Gwen said, "but it's all taken care of."

Gwen and Madelyn wandered like soulmates into the kitchen to put on a pot of tea. Ellis hung around the living room with Scott and Robbie, bemoaning the loss of Spencer and what it would mean to his judgeship. Robbie shot him a look of horror and ran outside.

Ellis shook his head after him. "The boy needs toughening up."

Between the drop-in visitors, there was the telephone. Cliff screened most of Gwen's calls. She insisted on taking the ones from her relatives in the East. Through it all, she maintained a composure that was to Scott a sign she'd not yet come to grips with the reality of Spencer's death. Although Jake and Scott agreed between themselves that Spencer had not died from natural causes, it was clear Gwen, who'd not known about the attempts on her husband's life, accepted this without question.

Scott worried about Jake, who acted as though Spencer's death had meant he'd failed some self-imposed test.

"Stop blaming yourself," Scott said when they were alone on the deck. "You couldn't have stopped it, no matter how he died."

The big man's eyes watered. "It was no heart attack. We both know that. It was also my job to keep him alive."

"I've had patients die on the operating table, and it always seemed I should have been able to prevent it, but I couldn't and you couldn't, either."

"Thanks, Doc," he said. But clearly he wasn't convinced.

"There's only one way you're going to jolt him out of it," Al observed later in the day when he and Scott were walking the dogs on the beach. "You've got to find out what—or who—killed Spencer. If it was suicide or a heart attack, then Jake's going to know it wasn't his fault."

"What makes you come up with suicide?"

"You said it. A possible drug overdose? What's that but suicide?"

Suicide hadn't even crossed Scott's mind, but clearly the idea wasn't original with Al. The afternoon news suggested he might have overdosed himself, theorizing he'd been despondent over recent sharp drops in his opinion polls.

Cliff took this hard. Calling it election-year slander, he got on the phone with his Washington contacts, uttering threats of lawsuits. Gwen quietly slipped out of the room.

Scott had expected Gwen to leave as soon as the funeral arrangements had been set, which Cliff took care of almost immediately. Burial at Arlington in a week's time. Services in Seattle after that. Scott was clearing the breakfast dishes when Gwen came out to ask if she could stay on a few extra days.

Cliff heard and didn't like it. "We need to get back," he said. "It's vitally important to put Spencer's affairs in order before the wolf pack moves in."

Gwen shook her head firmly. "I'm not ready to face it—not yet. Is it all right with you, Scottie?"

It was only the second time she'd called him Scottie. If she'd been restless and searching before, Spencer's death could only have made her more so. Erin was returning, and Scott didn't know how it would be between them, and here was Gwen complicating it, asking what might very well be misinterpreted.

"I just need some time," Gwen said, her eyes pleading for his understanding. "Do you mind awfully?"

"No—no, of course not."

She smiled her thanks and then to Cliff, she said, "You go on. I'll join you later."

Cliff's face darkened. "I think this is unwise, but if you're staying, then so am I."

Scott was much relieved.

After dinner, Scott found Jake on the beach, by himself, slumped against a log, looking out to sea. He would also stay on with Gwen, he said on the news. He showed little interest in the arrangements and appeared to have given up the idea of finding Spencer's killer. In some strange way, Spencer's death appeared to represent defeat for Jake.

Hoping to snap him out of his mood, Scott analyzed the circumstances that led to Spencer's death. "We looked for him on the beach and didn't find even a footprint."

"Tide was up," Jake said in a flat voice.

"But it's going out now, and Spencer had to have left by way of the beach and doubled back—or by boat—because the Secret Service people were watching the drive, and they didn't see anyone leave all night. Remember?"

Jake's eyes sharpened. "What are you trying to say?"

"That there must be something out there to tell us where he went, and maybe even with whom."

Jake agreed to join Scott on another search of the beach. They inspected every inch of the sand and crabgrass all the way to the lighthouse and found nothing. Any traces that might have been there clearly had been washed away with the tides.

"How about going north again?"

Jake shook his dark head in discouragement. "Don't see how it will help."

They trudged back toward the house, Dandy running ahead of them. By Goose Island, Dandy ran off toward the road.

"Saw a deer," Scott guessed, whistling after the dog.

Jake called, too, but the dog kept going.

They were walking over the grassy bank below Scott's deck when Dandy finally reappeared, dragging a long piece of cloth behind him.

Scott slipped the end of the rag out of the dog's mouth. "What have you found this time?" The cloth was soft and rubbery. It was wet from sea water, and a piece of green seaweed was wrapped around part of it.

"What is it?"

"An Ace bandage." Scott began to roll it up.

"Looks long enough to encase a mummy," Jake said.

24

The next morning Scott called Leroy for the lab findings.

"Normally, they'd be here in twenty-four hours," Leroy said. "But when a United States senator dies under unusual circumstances, they have to send it to the pathologist at Bethesda Naval Hospital in Maryland. Don't know when I'll have anything."

"Standard procedure," Scott said.

"Oh, we found out why Billy had it in for Bruner. It was the boat fire on Lopez. Billy had an option on one of the boats. A friend of his was living aboard, died in the fire. He got the notion Bruner set the fire."

"Did he?"

"Pretty hard to do. He was in Alaska at the time."

Disturbed and confused by his conversation with Leroy, Scott wandered into the kitchen. Gwen was there and she wanted to talk.

"Coffee?" she said, pouring him a cup.

He was puzzling the connection between Bruner and Spencer and not in a communicative mood, but clearly she needed someone, and he was it. He leaned against the counter and drank the coffee while she talked about the island, compared it to her life in the East. She was discontented with the nation's capital and all the parties, which surprised him because he thought that part of her life with Spencer would have appealed to her.

"You'd hate it, Scottie." She touched his arm, and he got the quivering sensations again. "Wouldn't it be fun to take the *Picaroon* out this afternoon? Just the two of us?" She edged so close her warm breath tickled his neck.

"I'd love to," he said, "but I'm meeting Erin at the airport."

"Erin," she said. "She's Professor Turner's granddaughter?"

"Yes."

She patted his shoulder. "Some other time then."

"It's a date."

She smiled, but there was disappointment in her eyes.

Cliff walked in on them, and Gwen began clearing dishes. "Morning," Scott said.

Cliff nodded sourly and walked out on the deck. Scott did the only thing he could think to do. He loaded Dandy into the Jeep and drove into Friday Harbor, hours ahead of Erin's flight.

He stopped by the barber's for a haircut, and then he and Dandy walked down the docks to see if Vic had gone fishing. He had. Next he dropped in at the Underwater Shop. The shop people still didn't connect the tank problem to Spencer, for which Scott was relieved. There were enough rumors floating around the island, as it was.

He left the shop and, on a hunch that had been growing since the night of the reception, went to the newspaper office.

"Barry Dickson?" the editor said. "Went down with the crab

boat that sank in the Bering Sea. Ten years or so ago, I think. Sure. We ran the story." He disappeared into the back rooms and after several minutes returned with a stack of old newspapers. "They ran investigations for months," the editor said. "Nothing came of it, but there were some big lawsuits. Owners settled out of court. They could afford it. Boat was insured to the hilt."

Scott thanked him and found a corner of the newsroom to read. It was all there, just as the editor had said. The boat had gone out in heavy seas and sank with three crewmen aboard, one of them Charleen's father, Barry Dickson. Investigators questioned the seaworthiness of the ship, but it had sunk in deep waters and salvage wasn't considered feasible. The owners, a limited partnership called Norfish Properties, recovered ten million dollars in insurance claims. The skipper, who reportedly had not gone with his crew that trip because of illness, was a man named Herm Bruner.

Spurred on, Scott asked the editor for the issue that carried the story of the Lopez fire. The editor dug it out, and Scott read. By the time he finished he had the beginnings of an idea how Bruner's death might be linked to Spencer's. Excited, he left the newspaper office and stopped to see Leroy, told him what he'd learned and what he suspected.

Leroy nodded thoughtfully. Then he deflated Scott completely. "I'll dig out what I can, but as far as I can see, it doesn't improve Billy's case one lick."

Dusk settled over the green slopes off Rocky Bay as Scott drove into the airport parking lot. He stood in the shelter of the hangars as the small plane flickered onto the runway. It had been three months since he'd seen Erin. There'd been many moments in that time when he'd ached to see her, to hear her laugh, to hold her. Now, as he waited, he wondered if it had been too long. If they would feel the same.

The plane touched down. The door opened, and the passengers started down the steps. Erin was the fourth one out. She walked

143

over to the wingtips, tall, slender, golden hair blowing in the wind. She held onto a two-suiter as she had that day by the ferry landing a year ago. She wore a pale-pink suit instead of the jeans, but otherwise looked exactly as she had when she'd entered his life at a critical point and changed it so completely.

She didn't see him at first as he started toward her. When she spotted him, the wonderfully vibrant smile lit up her face. He was at her side in a few long strides. "Scottie," she said, dropping the two-suiter and throwing her arms around his neck.

He kissed her. He hadn't realized until that kiss how *much* he'd missed her, and he put all his feelings into it. At first she returned it, a blissful moment. Then, nothing definite, just a subtle slipping away and, painfully, he knew. Things had changed between them.

"It's been a long time," she said. There was a nervousness in her laugh, as between strangers. She hugged Dandy, and the dog did one of the dances he reserved for special people. "It's so good to see you, too, Dandy, old boy." She roughed up his fur and didn't look up.

Scott picked up her luggage, and they started toward the Jeep. He reached with his free hand for hers, but she walked with both hands firmly planted in her jacket pockets.

Whatever the cause of this distance between them, she was as animated as ever. On the drive back to the Cape, she talked as fast as she could get the words out. Furniture markets were "all right." She didn't say when she was going back. She didn't mention her boss, this fellow Bob Finley. He didn't ask.

Between long side glimpses at her, he spent most of the drive answering her questions about Spencer and the murders. Her observations were, as always, intelligent and insightful, even if the subject wasn't the one he'd picked for their first meeting.

The idea of Billy killing anyone was ridiculous, and wasn't it strange, she said, that both Red and Bruner had a personal grudge against Spencer and then both were killed? And why had the killer sent threatening notes before Spencer was on the island to receive them? It was almost as though she wanted to take refuge behind the murders so they could have no discussions of a personal nature.

Al had dinner waiting. They ate spaghetti and garlic bread, Al's specialty, and jabbered about Spencer. With Al there, it was difficult to do otherwise anyway, and Scott resigned himself to it.

Erin picked up on things quickly. "Didn't you say Madelyn was one of the women Spencer dated that summer you worked as camp counselors on the island? Funny she wouldn't resent him if she knew about the others."

Scott nodded. "The one I always thought would resent his fickleness was Charleen's mother, Holly."

Erin pursed her lips in thought. "Does Charleen know her mother was involved with Spencer?"

"Interesting question. Of course, she was only seven or eight when her mother died."

"What sort of girl is she?"

"A squirrel," Al said.

Scott laughed. "She's conscientious. Vulnerable, I think."

Erin lifted an eyebrow, and Scott explained about Robbie's relationship with Charleen. Erin screwed her face up in disapproval. "You think he's using her?"

"He may be."

"Poor girl." She pondered a moment. "Do you think Robbie was aware of what was going on between his mother and Spencer?"

"I doubt it."

They finished dinner and took their coffee in the living room. Erin selected the chair by the fireplace. Scott sat on the sofa and looked across the room at her. Erin set her cup on the table beside her. Archimedes hopped onto her lap and purred loudly. Erin stroked the cat and didn't look up.

"Don't forget the wife," Al said, coming in with a fresh pot of coffee. "She'd be bound to resent his philanderings."

Erin lifted her head in interest. "What *about* his wife?"

Scott shook his head. "Gwen's not the type."

145

"Why?" Erin said.

"She's a very nice person, for one thing. Besides there's the bombs and the air tank. Hardly woman's work."

Erin grew quiet, but this stirred Al. "Proves nothing. You seen some of those sweet little things swinging picks and shoveling dirt at the dig?"

"Take my word for it, Al. It's not Gwen."

"Aren't you being overprotective?" Erin said.

Perhaps it was the accusation in her voice, or perhaps his conscience. The suggestion irritated him. "Why should I be?"

Erin's cheeks rose in color. "I don't know. Why are you?" Archimedes abandoned her lap.

"Mmmpf," Al said, and began clearing away the dinner dishes.

The old man clattered around the kitchen, and Erin stared bleakly at her cup. "I'm sorry. That was unfair."

Scott knelt beside her chair and placed a hand over hers. "Erin, I've missed you."

"You didn't call." Her lips formed a childlike pout.

"I called a dozen times. You weren't always there."

"You didn't write very often."

"I meant to. I thought about you all the time."

She looked down at her cup again, sitting untouched beside her, and Scott said, "What about this guy, Finley?"

"He's very nice."

There was something in her voice. Had she been wanting to tell him her future plans and hadn't known how to break it to him? He knew what he needed to ask, but couldn't bring himself to do it. If she'd decided to marry this Finley, he didn't want to know. If she'd decided to marry Finley, it wouldn't matter what he said.

Al walked back in, still talking about the murders. "What's hard to understand is how the killer got Spencer to the dig."

"By boat."

"Hit him on the head and dragged him there?"

"More likely, coaxed him. There were no bruises or contu-

146

sions. That's the problem with proving murder. No signs of a struggle."

"Stupid," Al said. "Why not dump him in the bay?"

"Wouldn't look like suicide."

"Probably *is* suicide. Spencer sure as the devil would've put up a fight if someone tried to stuff cocaine up his nose."

"Unless he couldn't struggle," Scott said.

"Isn't it funny," Erin said reflectively, "all the victims here were left helpless."

"What do you mean?" Al said.

"Well, you said both the fishermen had been drinking and they couldn't have put much of a fight, and, apparently, Spencer was doped."

From the kitchen, the phone rang. Al answered. "It's Leroy. Says he has news."

"You hit paydirt on that crab boat, Doc," Leroy said. "The Coast Guard confirmed it was one of the boats listed as lost in the Lopez fire."

"So Bruner wasn't the owner?"

"No. Belonged to a limited partnership. It was well insured with the rest of the boats. They collected big on it."

"Do you know who the partners are?"

"Uh-huh. Reads like a who's who."

"Was Spencer on the list?"

"No, but his wife was and several of their friends, including one of our local attorneys." Leroy read the names.

Scott sighed regrets. He'd hoped he'd been wrong. "Damn!"

"Oh, on those military records, they were all in the service, including Billy."

"I didn't ask about Billy."

"He was in the navy. One other interesting item. Jake was in the Special Services unit that attempted to rescue our hostages in Iran. Lost his only brother when the bomb he'd wired exploded prematurely from a faulty fuse."

So that was Jake's ghost.

"And Spencer Manning was the same senator who called for an investigation of the rescue operation. He called the participants incompetents—*his* words, not mine. It's all in the Congressional Record."

Scott began to see what Leroy was getting at and didn't like it. "Jake was on the boat with me, remember?"

"There was a farmer around here a few years ago. Shot his wife and kids, then shot himself. Police psychiatrists called it deep depression."

"And Jake defused the bomb," Scott reminded.

"Maybe he wanted to scare the senator to death. Or maybe he changed his mind. Uh-oh, long distance call coming in. Hang on."

He returned shortly. "That was the navy pathologist. You were right again. The senator died of an overdose of cocaine. Fact is, beginning to look like your ideas about this business were right on the money."

"Yeah," Scott said glumly, "but which one killed Spencer?" He was almost afraid to find out.

25

While Erin and Al listened in bewildered silence, Scott told them what he knew and what he suspected. "It goes back to the commercial fishing problems. Remember, Al, when the state and federal governments were so desperate to cut the number of boats fishing in the Inland waters they got the Congress to fund a buy-back program?"

Al nodded. "Knew some boys sold their boats to the state on that deal. Practically gave them away. State appraisers killed them."

"Why would the state want to buy the fishing boats?" Erin asked.

"To get the boat and the license out of the system."

"But what in the world did the state do with all those boats?"

"Sold them at auction."

Erin frowned. "Who would buy an unlicensed fishing boat?"

"Spencer and his partners."

"I can't think why."

"Because they knew they could turn right around and sell them to the Indians, who, you may recall, aren't bound by the state's licensure laws. They go by tribal laws."

"Why didn't the Indians buy directly from the auction?"

"I'm sure many did, but Spencer made it very attractive for them to buy from the partners by arranging low-cost government loans and subsidies. Spencer served on key committees on fishing and Indian affairs, remember, which gave him access to tribal counsels, state fisheries files. He knew which boats were to be auctioned, how they were equipped, their appraisals. The partners were able to buy these grossly underpriced boats and sell them for top market prices."

Al chuckled. "And by selling to the Indians the partners probably qualified for low-interest loans and didn't have to take cash from their own pockets."

"Not much anyway."

Al grew excited. "I can see all kinds of possibilities here. Tax write-offs . . ." He sucked thoughtfully on his pipe. "Mmm. Don't see how it ties to the fire, though. The buy-back program ended couple years ago."

"But Spencer still had access to boat transactions through the Department of Commerce. He knew when the fishermen bought new boats and sold their old ones. The state won't issue new licenses, remember, so the old boats automatically became unlicensed and not worth much on the open market."

"So the partners kept on buying and selling boats?"

Scott nodded. "Didn't make as much, but it was still a sweet racket."

"So what about the fire?" Erin asked.

"Someone saw a way to make more money. The boats were heavily insured. Didn't cost much to insure for those short periods before the sales were consummated, and with their own appraisers, the appraisals were always high."

Erin drew in her breath. "Bruner set the fire so they could collect the insurance!"

"He did more than that. He pulled one of the boats out of the pack first, ran it to Alaska, changed the document numbers, and insured it again. I think he was planning to sink it up there and claim the insurance a second time when the Coast Guard confiscated it. Bruner, you see, had some previous experience with sinking ships."

Scott explained his theory about the *Alaskan Star,* that Bruner had deliberately scuttled the *Star* for the insurance. "There were reports at the time of fishermen at sea hearing an explosion. He probably set a bomb in the hold and sent his crew out while he stayed ashore."

Erin shuddered. "How sick."

Scott nodded. "He wasn't a very nice fellow."

"So the partners got into the insure-'em-and-scuttle-'em business?" Al said.

"Not *all* the partners. Spencer wouldn't mind using his office for favors, hiding behind the others, but I think he'd draw the line at involvement in anything so risky as sinking ships where human lives were in jeopardy."

"You think Bruner acted on his own?"

"Not on his own. No! Bruner was only a silent partner. His problem was he got nervous. Think how he must have felt when the Coast Guard collected his boat, knowing it was only a matter of time before they tied it to the fire and then the old business about the *Star* would come out. And think how the killer must have felt, fearing Bruner was going to do something rash, maybe seek immunity, and drag them all into it."

"You're saying one of the others directed the whole operation?"

Scott nodded. "At least one."

"And did the killing?"

Scott sighed. "On this, I'm not sure."

Erin was looking fully unsatisfied when the phone rang. This time Scott answered.

It was Vic, and he was excited. "Talked to Mike. Now he says he saw *two* people come off Red's boat that morning."

"Was one a woman?"

"How did you know?"

"Psychic, I guess. Can he describe them?"

Vic hesitated. "Here's the thing. Mike can be a stubborn son of a bitch when he wants to. I think he's known all along what he saw, but doesn't want to get involved. What do you want me to do with him?"

"Convince him he's helping all the fishermen by remembering. Then tell him not to breathe it to anyone, except you."

"Okay. Oh, one other thing. I guess you know Billy's in the slammer again. Seems he was on the *Mollie O* before we found Bruner's body that day. Went there to talk, he says. Bruner was already dead and Billy didn't know how to tell Leroy without incriminating himself, so he worked the deal to get us over there. Dumb bastard!"

Scott remembered how nervous Billy had been that night.

"If we don't come up with something fast, he's a cooked goose, you know that, don't you, Doc?"

Back in the living room, Erin faced Scott with the question she'd clearly been stewing over while he was on the phone. "If you know who is committing these horrible murders, why don't you tell the sheriff?" She was still unhappy with him, he could see that, and he got no pleasure from the fact.

"I need proof." From what he was beginning to suspect, he wasn't sure he wanted to know.

She frowned impatience with his answer and loud staccato raps rattled the kitchen door. Both dogs started barking.

"What now?" Al sighed.

It was Charleen, trembling and frightened. Under the dim porchlight her eyes were dilated wildly. She looked beyond Al at Scott. "Dr. Eason?"

Scott had one of those bad feelings. "What's wrong?"

"It's Robbie. He went out to that boat. Said he'd be right back. That was ages ago."

Erin put an arm around her and drew her into the kitchen. "Come in and tell us about it."

Al watched with a raised eyebrow that said he didn't believe any of it.

Charleen looked suspiciously from one to the other of them and started to back up to the door. Scott caught her arm. "If Robbie is afraid the police are going to blame him for Spencer's murder, he needn't be."

Her face froze. "Why do you say that?"

"You're afraid Robbie will be implicated because he wrote the threatening notes to Spencer, but I know he wrote them under Spencer's orders."

Al and Erin gaped.

Charleen nodded vigorously. "It was the senator's idea. He told Robbie he needed to stir up public sympathy, that it was good publicity. But Robbie had no idea someone actually wanted to kill him."

"Did you know the police are calling the senator's death a suicide?" Al said.

Her eyes grew desperate again. "Robbie says it's murder. That's why he went to the boat, to get proof."

"What proof? What boat?"

"The ship's log that belonged to the crab fisherman."

"Bruner?"

She nodded. "It's the fishing boat anchored in Griffin Bay. Robbie saw the man who owns the boat in a tavern in Friday Harbor and thought it was safe to go out there and look for the log." She bit her lips. "But that was an hour ago."

"Don't worry," Scott said. "Davey Olson owns that boat, and

even if Davey finds Robbie prowling around, he might snap, but he won't bite."

Charleen screwed up her face in doubt, and Scott remembered she'd stopped at the house first. "Who else knows Robbie went out there?"

Charleen thought. "I guess I mentioned it to Mrs. Manning and the others."

Scott's pulse jumped. He flew to the phone, dialed Leroy. Leroy wasn't there. He left a message with the dispatcher and when he finished, said, "Al, do you think we could borrow John Edward's outboard?"

"Don't know why not. He's offered it to me dozens of times."

Scott started for the door. Dandy got up to follow. "You stay, boy."

Charleen started after him. "You're not going without me."

Erin slipped on her sweater. "We're *all* going."

"You can come as far as the creek, if you hurry," Scott said. He didn't tell them he was afraid they might already be too late.

26

All across Griffin Bay, the water was perfectly still. Dark clouds blotted out the moon. The only light came from the houses on the west shore and the occasional sweep of the airport beacon from Lopez Island. A gull cried. Then everything slipped into silence again.

Scott climbed into Webster's dinghy and instructed Al, "You stay here and wait for Leroy. When he comes, send him out."

"I think we should *all* wait until Leroy gets here," Erin said in an anxious voice.

Charleen stepped into the small boat. "I'm going!" She set her small mouth in a stubborn line.

153

Scott let out an exasperated sigh. "You want to get Robbie out alive?"

The suggestion shocked her. "What do you mean?"

"I mean I believe Robbie is in serious trouble, and we're wasting valuable time arguing about it. I'm going, and I'm going alone."

Charleen stepped out of the boat.

Erin started to say something, decided against it, and stood with her hands in her pockets, watching while Scott connected the gas line to the outboard.

Al shook his head. "He'll hear that engine before you get within a country mile."

Scott nodded agreement. "It's not far. I'll just use the oars."

Al gave the boat a shove. Scott pulled on the oars, and the boat slid away from the dock. As he stroked out of the creek, he heard Erin cry out softly, "Scottie, please be careful."

No tide to fight, Scott noted gratefully. He counted the strokes. Each one propelled him swiftly into Griffin Bay. Past the reef, he counted three sailboats and four small pleasure cruisers lying at anchor in a circle around the bay. A couple hundred yards farther out near the fish buyer's barge, the familiar silhouette of the *Mollie O* appeared out of the darkness.

Her lamps were dim as Scott approached. She swung quietly at anchor. Except for a faint light coming from the cabin porthole, there was no sign of anyone on board. Then he saw Robbie's skiff, a small dark shadow at the waterline along the *Mollie's* starboard rail.

The *Mollie's* cabin hugged the stern. The drum and nets, like a giant spindle of thread, sat from her midships forward. The roller was on the bow pulpit. It was a small cabin, as he remembered, not much room for three men facing each other with one of them intent on mayhem. But it looked like Robbie was alone. Scott's heartbeat returned to near normal. Maybe he'd worried for nothing.

He started around the bow, dipping the oars in gently so as not to slap water. He rounded the pulpit and almost rammed the second boat. It was tied to the port rail—small, well powered with a two hundred–horse outboard. He felt a quick flutter in his chest. Robbie had company.

He banked the oars and slid in on the starboard side. The *Mollie O* was a wood boat, probably displaced ten tons. He was grateful for every pound. She wasn't likely to bounce from a dinghy pulling alongside. He tied the line to the rail and considered what to do next.

No good way to get into that cabin. If he climbed aboard slowly, he'd chance making a noise, alerting them below. Forewarned, the killer would shoot. He cursed himself for not taking the time to retrieve his revolver from the house. As it was, he had only his two fists. Not much protection against bullets. He looked around the boat for a weapon. Nothing. The oars? He might use one as a club. He ran his fingers over the long paddle. Big and heavy. Too unwieldy. Surprise was his only weapon, he decided.

He crouched in readiness and began to count. He counted to seven, and suddenly the cabin lights went out. No more time. His breathing came in constricted puffs as he swung over the rail, dropped onto the deck, landed lightly. He took two quick strides and burst into the cabin.

Glittering black eyes stared back at him. It was dark, but not so dark he couldn't recognize the face, shaped so much like Spencer's except for the glasses still perched forward on his nose. It was Cliff, and he wasn't holding a gun. Good, Scott thought, breathing easier. We start even. Then he saw the flash of a blade in Cliff's right hand. It was long and sharp as a butcher's knife. On the floor, Robbie lay face down, not moving. Scott went cold all over.

Cliff acted first. He kicked the door shut. Scott's heart thumped crazily as he realized his mistake. He'd locked himself into a six-foot-square box with a man who'd killed three times already and would hardly hesitate to kill again.

"You shouldn't have come," Cliff said in a deadly calm voice. He raised his hand and, with it, the knife.

155

Scott looked swiftly around the room. There were the faint remains of a fire going in the wood stove. Its dimming embers provided the room's only light. On the stove top, a kettle of water sent up a spray of steam. Scott took a step and banged against a big metal pot. It clanked like cymbals crashing together. Cliff jumped, alarm written all over his face. Not smart to upset a killer.

"Don't move," Cliff snapped, brandishing the knife.

Scott nodded obediently. The floor around him was littered with pots, boots, kitchen utensils, and other assorted gear. Cliff had been searching for the log.

"I knew it," Cliff said. "I knew you'd be the one person who'd figure it out." Silver flashed again in the faint glow from the stove.

"Don't be a fool. The sheriff's on his way right now."

Cliff's laugh said he was confident, enjoying himself. "I talked to the sheriff's office before I left the house. He won't be back for hours. But when he gets here he'll find Spencer's killer dead and you beside him, killed trying to bring him in."

"Leroy will never believe that."

Cliff laughed again, and Scott thought, He's right. It's exactly what Leroy might think. Robbie wrote the notes. Charleen put the kids up to the cherry bomb. Both Charleen and Robbie had reason to want Spencer dead. If Leroy talked to Vic's friend from Alaska, he'd figure it out that it was Robbie and Charleen who'd paid Red a visit just before Cliff killed him, that they'd come trying to find out about the log. Unfortunately for Red, he'd refused to talk to them.

Cliff flexed his wrist so the tip of the knife pointed at Scott's chest. Scott's heart pumped so loud he could hear it. His blood raced through his veins so swiftly he felt lightheaded. The cabin was much too small for maneuvering. Cliff had the knife, and it was only a matter of a quick thrust into the spleen or another vital organ, and it would be all over.

A spleen ruptured in the right place could cause a man to bleed to death in a few moments. Scott thought of the victims of knifings in his residency days. More often than not it was too late before they ever reached the ER. Here, in the middle of the bay, with no one near enough to hear his shouts from inside the cabin, there'd be no chance at all. What was worse, Cliff killing him and making it look as though Robbie had done it would leave Cliff completely free—free to go after Gwen, free to keep his profits from the partnership, free to kill again.

Scott's mind worked double time. Behind Cliff, the door was shut. Beside Scott was the wheel, and on the starboard bulkhead, a cabinet and the stove. It was the stove Scott thought about as he started talking.

"You've been very clever," he said in as calm and pacifying a voice as he could manage, considering he was scared near speechless by the ice in Cliff's eyes. Cliff was a pathological killer who was capable of the worst brutality. "You threw suspicion off yourself by making it look like the killer mistook you for Spencer."

"So you knew about my concussion?"

"I wasn't sure, but it struck me strange there wasn't more injury to the tissue."

"That was the kid. I talked him into hitting me with a piece of wood—not hard—just enough to make it look like another attempt on Spencer's life, but he did such a rotten job of it, I had to club myself with a rock. Then I took a propranolol."

Scott nodded. "A beta blocker will drop your blood pressure. Good touch."

Cliff smiled pleasure with himself. "And you did the rest."

Yes, Scott thought, silently cursing his stupidity.

"Would've worked, too, if the kid hadn't started asking questions." He brought the knife up, and Scott thought fearfully, He's tired of talk.

"But why kill Bruner? He was your partner."

"He went chicken on me. I couldn't tell what he might do."

Scott nodded. "And then Spencer discovered you were behind the fire on Lopez and threatened to expose you. Right?"

Cliff laughed. "Wrong. Spencer didn't know from straight up."

"But he guessed."

157

"He was starting to ask too many questions."

"And there was Gwen . . ."

It was the wrong thing to say. Cliff's mouth curled up cruelly, and now he looked like the killer he was—cold, face torn up with the most incredible hate. He started toward Scott. He measured his steps. Even in anger, Cliff was a precise man.

Scott slid another inch toward the stove. Too slow. Cliff lunged. It was a straight hard thrust, struck deep. Sharp pain traveled up and down Scott's arm. He stumbled back against the cabinet, bleeding all over his shirt. Cliff fell on top of him, still holding onto the knife, which was sticking out of Scott's shoulder. Cliff yanked, and the blade came out, ripping like the teeth of a chain saw on its way. The pain was excruciating. Scott sank dizzily to the floor and watched his blood flow. He caught hold of the wheel, hung onto it like a drunk for support, tried to pull himself back up, tried not to pass out.

His shoulder throbbed. Cliff laughed and came at him again. He took his time, and Scott thought, The next strike he'll go for pay dirt. The next thrust will hit a vital organ and finish the job. The room was small, but now the stove was out of reach. If only he could stay on his feet.

He waited helplessly for Cliff to come, felt the fury of those fierce eyes, thinking, He's going to do it now. Another second ticked off, and Scott thought, Sadistic bastard, he's enjoying this to the full. Another heartbeat. The blade went up, glittered in the light of the flames. Scott kicked. Caught Cliff in the knees. Cliff fell forward, and the blade zipped by Scott's ear, lodged in the wood behind Scott's head.

"Dirty bastard," Cliff said savagely as he worked to pull the knife free. "Son of a bitch!" He tugged frantically on the black handle, tugged until it worked loose. Knife raised, he hovered over Scott's wounded shoulder and smiled. His arm went up again.

Scott tried to shield himself. No use. It went in and out like a hot poker, burned raw tissue, leaving muscle and nerves exposed. Scott fell moaning to the floor. Cliff raised the knife one more time. Scott crawled to his knees, head spinning, heard that sinister laugh. There was the flash of steel and the determined set of Cliff's mouth. This time it was for keeps.

Scott fought off waves of lightheadedness. The room moved. Everything dimmed out. The arm went up. Scott leaped, almost fell on the stove. Plate was hot. Barely felt it. He got hold of the kettle with his good hand. Threw it. Boiling water showered the cabin.

Cliff's screams shattered the air. He fell to the floor, clawing at his face and screaming in agony as the scalding water seared his flesh. Woozily Scott slumped beside him, thinking vaguely, I've got to get the knife. Got to get out of here. Blood puddled up on the floor underneath him. He heard Cliff's agonizing cries and then the sound of boots thumping on the deck, and then—nothing.

27

Bright lights blazed. Behind them, white gowns and the fuzzy outline of a face. Cool fingers touched Scott's wrist. "Where am I?" Scott said in a thick tongue.

The face smiled. "You're in the recovery room of Bellingham General Hospital. You've just come out of surgery."

Scott touched his shoulder, felt only layers of gauze. Fear stirred slowly in his dulled brain. He raised his head anxiously. "M-my arm?"

The nurse laid reassuring hands on his chest. "It's numb from the anesthetic, but don't worry. Dr. Bruce does excellent work."

Through blurred eyes, Scott looked at the bandaged shoulder and the arm that hung in a sling across his chest, the tubes coming from his wrist and side. It was all too familiar. Only this time *he* was the patient, and it was *his* arm. Wanted to say something. Words wouldn't come.

"The drugs will make you sleepy for a while," the nurse said, "but that's what you need, lots of rest."

"Umm," Scott murmured, and the room faded out.

He woke again to pain. It traveled down his neck to his chest and across to his good arm. Sympathetic response. It hurt like the very devil. He lay on his back, arms and neck aching, and a voice faintly familiar said, "You pick the damnedest ways to get out of working."

Scott blinked, and the round face came into focus. It was his partner, Ralph Nelson, portly, prematurely balding, smiling at him with a sweetness that was fully out of character. Scott felt the beginnings of panic. *He wants to tell me I've lost the use of my arm.*

"Four weeks. That's how long they tell me you'll be basking in the sun while you nurse that shoulder back to health. You lucky bastard, you."

"It *will* go back to normal?"

Ralph's round face pinked. "Of course. What the hell you think? Some therapy, sure, but good as new."

Scott managed a smile. "I only asked."

"Stupid question. You know I'd tell you—" Ralph blustered.

Scott tried to raise his head. A sharp stab of pain went up and down his side. "Excuse me if I don't get up," he said, and fell back onto the bed.

Ralph studied the IV stand by Scott's head and then huddled with the nurse. "He's hurting," Scott heard him tell her. They started fooling around with the PCA box. Patient-controlled analgesia. Do-it-yourself pain medication.

"No!" Scott protested loudly. "Don't need anything."

Ralph walked back to his side and laid a hand on Scott's good shoulder. His face had the weary look Scott had seen on himself after the really long surgeries. There was concern in his eyes, as well. "Now, you listen to me. That little scuffle with the knife

160

lost you three units of blood, collapsed your lung, and came within an eyelash of cutting a major artery. As it was, it tore hell out of your muscle wall. The wonder is you still have an arm. You're going to hurt. Your PCA is for pain. Use it!"

Scott managed a half grin. "Thought the surgeon on the case was a guy named Bruce."

"I'm consultant. Now shut up and let us do our job," Ralph said gruffly.

The nurse pushed the button on the hand pump that lay beside Scott on the bed, and the painkillers began flowing through Scott's veins. Ralph patted Scott's good hand. "Take it easy, boy. I'll see you later."

It was a long night. Antiseptic smells. Nurses floated in and out, checked his pulse, fooled with the IV. Feet clicked on the tiled halls. Doctors conferred in whispers. Moaning from the room next door. Between short periods of sleep, Scott thought about Robbie. By dawn the drugs wore off, and the pain, now a dull ache, served as a reminder that Robbie was dead. It seemed wrong to spare himself pain. He did not use the PCA.

Breakfast consisted of watered-down orange juice, lukewarm mush, tea, and a poached egg. Scott poked his fork at the egg lying limp in its puddle of water and shoved the tray away.

It was raining outside, a real summer storm with black clouds. Scott thought about Robbie again, and regrets piled up like the raindrops sliding down the pane.

The nurse bustled in, clucked her tongue over the uneaten breakfast, and announced he had a visitor.

Jake walked in, looking fully relaxed and in a jubilant mood. He was flying back to Washington with Gwen the next morning.

"How's she doing?"

"She's weathering it very well. She knew nothing about any of it, of course."

"I know." It still troubled him that he'd doubted, that until he'd faced Cliff he'd not been sure. Gwen was a part of all this that bothered him deeply. Spencer had put her in as a silent partner, as usual with no regard to the consequences for her.

"Oh, about Dandy. The professor's taking care of him."

Scott nodded gratefully.

"And Gwen said she'd collect the sail some other time. I suppose you know what she means?"

Scott moved his head up and down, a little too emphatically. Pain stabbed his shoulder. He bit down, and Jake frowned.

"Hurt much?"

"Only when I move."

"You looked much worse last night."

"I imagine I did."

Jake settled in a chair and continued to look sympathetic. "You don't remember?"

"Not a thing after I threw the boiling water at Cliff."

"You did a good job of that."

"Seemed the only thing to do at the time," Scott said regretfully.

"Don't sweat that one. If you hadn't put him out of commission, neither you nor Robbie would be here to tell about it."

The words hung there, sinking in slowly. "Robbie's alive?"

Jake looked puzzled. "Didn't you *know*?"

Scott shook his head. "I was so sure — the way he lay there . . ."

"He's fine. That is, he will be. He lost a lot of blood. But he's a tough kid. He'll make it." Then Jake told how Erin had decided not to wait for Leroy and went to the house for help. "I knew something was wrong when Cliff ducked out of there after the girl. We commandeered a boat from one of the neighbors and went out on the *Mollie O*."

"Did you have any trouble with Cliff?"

"Not in his condition. We flew you and Robbie here. The sheriff sent Cliff to a Seattle hospital under police guard." Jake chuckled. "The media's having a field day. Now they're saying Cliff used his position of trust to make big bucks in an insurance fraud. They say the senator found out and was going to blow the whistle on him when Cliff killed him." It made Spencer and the partners, victims, rather than co-conspirators. Scott was grateful for Gwen's sake.

162

Jake paused in his revelations. "You know, don't you, that the senator set the partners up in the boat-buying business?"

Scott nodded. "A clear violation of the Senate Ethics Act. He probably put it together about the fire, too, but didn't have the courage to act on it."

Jake nodded. "I wish he'd come to me."

"He didn't want to tell anyone for fear of incriminating himself." Scott lifted the water glass from the table beside him and drank. It was warm and tasted like minerals.

Jake laughed. "Pretty bad, huh?"

"Had worse in the navy. Did Leroy find Bruner's log?"

"Uh-huh. In the fish box in the bilge." Jake strolled over to the window. Outside the sky was dark as night. "Bruner put it all down about the fire, everything. Named Cliff, didn't mention the senator."

"The night in the tavern before the blockade, Red talked about that log. Robbie heard and so did everyone else in the room. Robbie probably told Cliff. At the time he had no idea what he'd told him. Probably thought it had something to do with the notes the two were leaving around, and he wanted to protect Spencer. Who more logical to tell than the senator's trouble-shooter? Bad luck for Red."

Jake shook his head. "Robbie sure got himself into a pile of trouble working for the senator."

It was what bothered Scott the most. Spencer had cheated and abused his office, but more unforgivable was what he'd done to those who'd loved him—Robbie, Madelyn, Holly, Gwen. Even Cliff had probably been a serious young man with talent and promise until he hooked up with Spencer and learned how to take shortcuts. Psychiatrists would say the seeds of the psychopath had been there all along, but, surely, it had taken a catalyst like Spencer to set it off, for Cliff had been driven by the desire to prove his intellectual superiority. He'd hated Spencer for the power he held, hated writing his speeches, being his brains while Spencer took the bows, hated watching Spencer cheat on Gwen.

163

Jake continued to stand by the window. Scott thought he knew what still bothered him. "You must know by now it wasn't your fault. Not with Spencer or your brother."

Jake turned. Tears glistened in the corners of his eyes. He nodded slowly. "Sure, I know that, Doc. It just takes awhile for the hurt to go away."

After he left, the nurse walked in and started fooling around with the pillows. The pain had returned, and Scott felt restless.

"They're fine as they are," he protested.

"For your information, you have another visitor. So look sharp."

"I'm doing my best," Scott said unenthusiastically.

The nurse surveyed his face. He'd looked in the mirror and he knew he was a mess. He needed a shave, had a couple of mean bruises under his eyes where he'd hit the corner of the bunk. "I guess there isn't much you can do," she said, and left.

The door opened again, and Erin walked in, her golden hair falling gently to her shoulders. She was wearing the same pink suit she'd arrived in, and her face was pale and anxious. He tried to boost himself up. Sharp pain reminded him of his shoulder. He slipped back down just in time to receive her kiss.

"Scottie, darling," she murmured. "Waited all night to do this."

"If you waited that long," he said, breathing in the sweetness of her perfume, "the least you can do is do it right."

She laughed and kissed him a longer kiss. He put his good arm around her. His shoulder hurt like the devil. He didn't care. "I love you," he said. Surprised he had actually got out the words he'd wanted to say these past many months, he said it again.

Color bloomed in her cheeks, and he imagined she wasn't averse to the idea. It was much superior to the PCA box. His pain melted away. He was still kissing her when Al walked in.

Al took one look at them and shook his head. "Mmpf. Doctors say you could've bled to death."

"You're a cheery bear."

"Darned fool thing to do, going off alone that way."

Scott laughed and Erin joined in. They seemed unable to do anything else, which only annoyed the old man the more. Finally he insisted on knowing what had happened, and Scott told him.

"How did Cliff meet up with Bruner?" Al asked.

"Cliff set up the boat deal for the partners, picking the right people to handle the boats. Bruner was a natural for what Cliff had in mind."

"How did he sweet-talk Spencer into leaving his bed in the middle of the night? And don't tell me he just walked him to the dig, stuffed powder up his nose, and dumped him in a hole."

"Not quite. He waited until Jake was asleep. Jake's a sound sleeper. Then he woke Spencer to tell him he knew who set the bombs, or something like that. Whatever he said, he got Spencer to follow him to the beach. He had a boat waiting. Only way they could've gone without being seen by the guards. It was probably after they reached the dig that Cliff caught Spencer off guard, wrapped an Ace bandage around his arms, which acted like a straightjacket. After that, it was easy enough to overdose him with cocaine, leaving no injuries to the skin. Spencer just went to sleep. Essentially, that's what happens with an overdose of cocaine. It anesthetizes the victim, much as a vet puts down a dog or cat, and leaves everyone to conclude suicide or that the person was hooked on drugs and miscalculated."

"But why take him so far?"

"He had to get him away from the house or take the chance of being seen. He probably borrowed the Walters' runabout. They've been off island for months. Then he banked the boat by Henry's Point earlier in the evening. It would be completely out of sight, hidden by the jetty. He and Spencer had a short walk up the beach, perfectly natural, hidden by the logs and rocks, and if anyone had spotted them, it was just Spencer and his publicity man out discussing campaign problems. Anyway, once he got him to the dig, he overpowered him, drugged him, and left him there. He returned the boat to the Walters' place and walked back along the beach to his bed.

"Risky," Al said.

"He was a risk taker."

"Clever, too."

"He was a very clever man."

"What a waste," Erin said. "You know for a while I had an idea it might be Charleen who'd killed Spencer. She acted so strange. I was sure she was leading you into a trap."

"I have to admit it crossed my mind, too."

Al studied him with one of those catty smiles. "So you noticed the resemblance of the girl to Spencer?"

Scott nodded. "Particularly the night of the reception. It gave her motivation."

"There were rumors that Barry had married Charleen's mother to give the child a name," Al said. "The question is, did Charleen know Spencer was her natural father?"

"I think she did," Scott said. "I believe she deliberately hung around Robbie to get close to Spencer. I think she only hoped to embarrass Spencer, to get even, but when she met him succumbed to the Manning charm and backed off."

Erin stroked the bedsheets thoughtfully. "Scott, do you think—is it possible Spencer knew, too?"

"I wondered about that. He had an expression on his face when he saw her that night, all dressed up, looking so much like him. I was almost certain he knew, and I had the weirdest notion that maybe Gwen did, too."

"How must Charleen feel?" Erin said. "Both her parents gone, the horrible way Spencer died?"

"I think she has a better memory of Spencer than she might have if he'd lived."

Al nodded agreement. "What about Billy?"

"He's in the clear."

"What about the money?"

"Cliff took it from Red after he killed him and planted it on Billy's boat. Remember, Cliff had been nosing around all week before Spencer arrived. Knowing Billy's vulnerability, he went to a good deal of trouble to make the murders look like Billy had committed them in a drunken rage. But, as Erin pointed out, they were calculated crimes."

"When did I say that?" Erin said.

"When you remarked that in each case the victim was helpless. Red and Bruner were drunk. Spencer was doped."

Scott had been talking almost continuously for the past half hour and suddenly he felt weary. He leaned back against the pillow. Erin's face showed immediate concern. "Grandpa, we have to go. Scott needs rest."

Scott shook his head. "You only just got here."

The door opened, and a young nurse walked in and looked at them uncertainly. "Bathtime, Doctor."

"No," Scott said.

The nurse looked unsure.

"Don't worry," Erin said. "We're leaving."

"I don't want you to go," Scott said.

"Don't be a baby."

"Two more minutes."

Shaking his head in disgust, Al walked out. The nurse slipped out behind him.

Erin turned accusing eyes on Scott. "What is it that couldn't wait?"

He caught her hand and pulled her down on the bed beside him. "What about Dallas?"

"What about it?"

"When are you leaving?"

She smiled impishly and kissed him again, a long, highly satisfying kiss. "I'm not going," she murmured. "Didn't you know?"

"Do you mind," he said, "doing that again?"

The following day, Scott won walking privileges. Robbie was sitting up when Scott stepped into the room.

"Doc!" Robbie said cheerfully. "They said you were here."

167

Then he saw Scott's shoulder all trussed up in the sling and acres of gauze, and his smile died. "They said you were okay."

"I *am* okay."

Robbie frowned doubtfully. "If you're hurt, it's my fault."

"Wrong! Because of you, Cliff is behind bars."

Robbie looked glumly at the bed covers. "Maybe you didn't know I was the stupid jerk who put the dead fish on your bed."

"I know. And you wrote the notes. Forget it. I have."

"What about the sheriff?"

"I'm sure as far as Leroy is concerned, the case is closed."

Robbie shook his head in self-recrimination. "I thought the idea was stupid from the start, but I did it because the senator asked me to. His campaign needed a boost, and, well, you know the rest."

Scott sat on the bed beside the long lump made by Robbie's legs. "Spencer was a very persuasive person."

"Tell me about it!" He thumped his fist at the mattress, and Scott guessed he had more on his mind. "Cliff said the senator knew about that fire, that he didn't care if someone was killed because they got all that insurance money."

"I don't think you believe that any more than I do."

He nodded. "Yeah, but the senator was the kind of person who didn't care what he did to people as long as he got where he wanted to be. He used me and my mom and dad, and I thought he was so darned smart, and I used Char." He heaved a giant sigh, and Scott realized that whatever Charleen knew about her parentage, she hadn't told Robbie.

"How *is* Char?"

Robbie brightened. "Terrific. I mean, she was pretty upset about Spencer's death—that's the kind of person she is, caring, you know—but she's fine now."

Scott had been worried about the boy, that he might go on seeing Spencer as a role model, taking shortcuts himself, but clearly he'd done a lot of growing up in the past forty-eight hours.

"As for the senator . . ." Robbie shook his head. "I'm sorry what happened to him, but let's face it, Doc, no matter how you cut it, he wasn't much, was he?"

168